Murder at Mincing Manor

A Nancy Boys Mystery

by Michael Simon
and Richard Simon

A SAMUEL FRENCH ACTING EDITION

SAMUEL FRENCH

FOUNDED 1830

New York Hollywood London Toronto

SAMUELFRENCH.COM

ISBN   978-0-573-69559-9   Printed in U.S.A.   #15282

Murder at Minsing Manor: a nancy boys mystery was first presented in New York by the Ridiculous Theatrical Company, Everett Quinton, Artistic Director. The production opened at The Actors' Playhouse on October 24, 1995 with the following cast:

Bob Anderson	Cory Lippiello
Buddy Brady	Chista Kirby
Marius Mintsingue, Buck Arnge	Grant Neale
Glory Holden	Everett Quinton
Pig Marrano	Jason Williams
Zarah Zine	Lenys Samà
Father Pat, Mr. Anderson	Kyle Kennedy
Officer Joe	Tom Deroesher
Marty	Dave Murray
Eddie	Wilfredo Medina

The production was directed by Chuck Brown, with Set by Tom Greenfield, Costumes by Kaye Voyce, Lighting by Richard Currie, Sound by Raymond D. Schilke, Wigs and Make-up by Zsamira Ronquillo. The production Stage Manager was Bill Nobes, and the Managing Director of the Ridiculous Theatrical Company was Adèle Bové.

CAST OF CHARACTERS

BOB ANDERSON: A pubescent boy, shy, intelligent, sensitive. Played by a woman.

BUDDY BRADY: Attractive, slightly younger. His voice cracks in the most outrageous way possible. Also played by a woman.

MARIUS MINTSINGUE: Like Vincent Price, only effeminate.

GLORY HOLDEN: Mintsingue's apparent wife, a husky hairy man in drag. Imagine W.C. Fields thinking he's Mae West.

PIG MARRANO: A big, strong stupid guy with shoulderpads. The muscle of the operation.

ZARAH ZINE: The half-man/half-woman from a side show. The male half (left side of body) is a gentleman of the Ronald Coleman variety; the female half (right side) is French and very feminine. (When not noted in direction as "(MALE)", she is speaking in her female persona.)

FATHER PAT: Standard Irish stage brogue.

OFFICER JOE: The model of New York's finest.

MARTY and EDDIE: Attractive, obnoxious punks of the Dead End Kids variety. Marty is the weaselly one, Eddie the dumb one. One may wear a cap, the other a Jughead hat.

MR. ANDERSON, T.V. ANNOUNCER: Offstage voices.

BUCK ARNGE: F.B.I. man. Same actor who plays Mintsingue, minus old age make-up.

Scene

Levittown, U.S.A. The Mintsingue family home and (briefly) the Anderson living room.

Time

Roughly 1954, outrageous anachronisms notwithstanding.

For C.L.
homo ludens
in heaven

and
to hardy girls
and nancy boys
everywhere

ACT I

Scene 1

SETTING: The main room at Mintsingue Manor, a combination of Gothic horror and pastel kitsch: Ozzie and Harriet meet the Addams Family. Exits to the kitchen, a stairwell, a closet, the boudoir (alternatively referred to as bedroom or chamber), and the front entrance. The arrangement may be, SL to SR, a window, the door to the boudoir (alternatively referred to as bedroom or chamber), closet door, front door, stairwell, swinging kitchen door, bar. Portraits of Mintsingue and Holden in their youth, looking like Oscar Wilde and Gertrude Stein, respectively. A chaise longue and a tête-à-tête.

(AT RISE: Friday night. Thunder and lightning give way to rain. A spotlight illuminates BUDDY and BOB, two young adolescent boys in pajamas, sitting on sleeping bags, watching a horror movie on an invisible TV placed over the audience, and eating cereal; several cereal boxes are nearby, as is a sugar bowl and a small pile of magazines. We hear horror movie music, roars, and screams; a climactic moment in the flick.)

(Elsewhere on stage, another spot illuminates MARIUS MINTSINGUE. He plays to an invisible camera, also placed above the audience. He is standing on a chair, a noose around his neck.)

9

MARIUS. That wasn't so very frightful, was it? I'm sure we all confront more horrifying moments every day. And cope with them... as best we can! I hope you'll *hang around* for this word from our sponsor.

(Light dims on MINTSINGUE. In the shadows, GLORY and PIG can be seen helping him out of the noose and into his next gimmick. Commercial music at low volume, so as not to obscure the following exchange.)

BOB. Jumps off chair, hangs by neck.
BUDDY. Got it.

(Writes on tablet.)

MR. ANDERSON. *(Offstage.)* Are you watching that fruity show again?
BOB. *(Quietly.)* It's a great show.
MR. ANDERSON. *(Offstage.)* A little fresh air won't kill you, ya know!
BOB. It's dark out, Dad.
MR. ANDERSON. *(Offstage.)* If you'd spend a little time learning to throw a football around and not cooped up in front o' that boob tube all day...
BUDDY. But Bob doesn't like football, Mr. Anderson.
MR. ANDERSON. *(Offstage.)* I thought you were gonna learn him tuh.

(Spot hits MINTSINGUE, staggering, a bloody dagger in his chest.)

MARIUS. I'd like to thank our sponsor for that... heartfelt message. I hope you'll find the rest of the show equally horrible!!

(Spot out on MINTSINGUE. GLORY and PIG help him into the iron maiden.)

MR. ANDERSON. *(Offstage.)* If he's so great at dying, how come he keeps coming back every week?

BOB. Da-ad! *(To BUDDY.)* Dagger in chest.

BUDDY. Check. Didn't that little guy get a dagger in his chest in *House of Hemoglobin*?

BOB. Peter Lorre, yeah. *(Writes.)* But Peter Lorre wasn't in *Mutilation on Lonely Street.* That was Elisha Cook, Jr.

MR. ANDERSON. Well I've had it. I'm going upstairs.

BOB. Good night, Dad.

MR. ANDERSON. And go to sleep!

(We hear ANDERSON stomping off. More movie music, roars, and screams. BOB is staring at BUDDY.)

BUDDY. What're you starin' at?

BOB. *(Turns away.)* Whaddaya want next?

BUDDY. Whaddaya have again?

BOB. Hold on. *(Reads boxes.)* Okay, we got Sucrosonic Jet Flakes, Buzz Bombs—

BUDDY. Frosted Buzz Bombs?

BOB. ... uh-huh, uh, Corpus Crispies... *(Looks in box.)* Yuck! Double-Glaze Sugar Slabs...

BUDDY. Double-Glaze *Super* Sugar Slabs?

BOB. No, just the regular ones. *(BUDDY shrugs.)* ... Syrup-

Coated Mini-Cakes, and, uh, Spastix.

BUDDY. Which one has the best prize?

BOB. I already took out all the prizes, you doofus.

BUDDY. Oh. Whadja get?

BOB. Uh, this one, nothing, invisible ink; this one, nothing, bloody eyeball; Buzz Bombs, severed finger, totally fake. I'm sending away though.

BUDDY. What're you getting?

BOB. *(Excited.)* Well, for forty Buzz Bombs, you get a Captain Benzene ray gun.

BUDDY. *(Reading.)* Hey, for 60 Jet Flakes you get the combination chattering teeth, undulating tongue, and spastic colon.

BOB. *(Shrugs.)* Raygun's better. *(They pour cereal and eat, regularly glancing at screen. Sugar Slabs are clearly rectangular "cubes" of sugar.)* That is so fake.

BUDDY. I'll say.

BOB. I mean, that's just a guy in a rubber costume.

BUDDY. Yeah. Who do they think they're fooling? I like it better when they use real monsters. Hey, Bob. Still got those Playboys your dad gave ya?

(BOB takes out magazines--Playboys for BUDDY, a muscle mag for BOB.)

BOB. I got you a new one. *(They begin reading.)* Wow. These guys sure have good builds, huh?

BUDDY. *(Glancing over.)* No kidding! Like Superman-- Bam! Pow! *(Goes back to heavy breathing over the Playboy. Silence.)* Wow. Get a load of Miss July. She's beautiful!

(Silence. More eating and TV-watching.)

BOB. You really like those... Sugar Slabs?

BUDDY. Yeah, they're great!

BOB. It's a kids' cereal!

BUDDY. Is not!

BOB. Is too--it doesn't have any sugar on the outside. Just glaze.

BUDDY. Sugar Slabs has sugar on the inside, but then you get to decide how much you put on the outside. Freedom of choice!

BOB. Oh, brother! *(During the following dialogue they take turns dousing cereal with sugar in exponentially increasing quantities, as if trying to outdo each other, periodically tasting and adding still more. BOB'S eyes drift back to muscle magazine. BOB shows magazine to BUDDY. Carefully)* Boy, wouldn't you like to look like this?

BUDDY. Huh? *(Then looks over.)* Oh, I'll say! We'd be real men,then. Hey, what's that thing he's wearing?

BOB. It's a posing strap. They wear it so you can see the definition of the musculature.

BUDDY. Hm. Looks like a diaper! *(Silence. Reading. Both increasingly aroused, regularly glancing at TV screen. Something on the screen catches BOB'S eye.)* These girls sure are pretty. No pimples or bumps or anything.

BOB. They airbrush them.

BUDDY. Oh. That would hurt.

BOB. *(Pause.)* Hey. You want to, uhh... *(Trails off.)*

BUDDY. Uh. Okay.

(BOB begins to masturbate BUDDY enthusiastically, BUDDY continues to look at the Playboy, but begins to masturbate BOB to be fair, and to keep BOB going. They hold position,

eyes glued to the screen. They continue eating cereal, sugar, gazing at magazines, glancing at TV, and masturbating with increased frenzy. As BUDDY and BOB approach climax, the television suddenly increases in volume.)

BOB. He's gonna go in that room and get his head ripped off.

BUDDY. How do you know? Oh, he is.

BOB and BUDDY. Don't go in that room! Don't go in there! Don't go in there!

(Both scream and come. Ending music. Lights on MINTSINGUE in coffin.)

MARIUS. Thank you for joining me for another FRIGHT-FUL feature of Fear Theatre. In a moment, you will see the final clue in our creepy creature contest. But now, alas, the time has come for me to take a much needed sojourn from this oh so cru-el world. I needs must entrust myself to the arms of Somina, the goddess of sleep; sip of the nectar of Opius, god of dreams. I yearn to wrap myself tight in the tenebrous counterpane of Nocturna, deep in the vale of Valius. In my next incarnation, I'll be in Hollywood California, filming the cinematic epic *Palace of Plasma.* For the nonce, I bid you *au revoir,* as I slip into my lovely Iron Maiden for the profoundly penetrating pleasure of its razor-sharp spikes harrowing my flesh and piercing my eyes. Don't be dismayed as the billows of my fresh scarlet blood flow gently from the casket. I hope you have--pleasant dreams! Wa-ha-ha-ha-ha...! *(GLORY and PIG pull visible invisible wires, close casket.)* MMM... OO. Ouch... Hey... What... the ... AAAArrrrrrgggghhhhh!!!!!!!!

(Spot out on MINTSINGUE.)

BUDDY. That was great!
BOB. That's the coolest one ever!!!
BUDDY. Look at the blood!

(TV screen fades, generic television noises in background. Boys cleaning themselves up.)

JOE. *(V.O.)* Hey, kiddos. It's your old pal Officer Joe, with another tip from the pages of... Crimestopper's Notebook! Before you get into a car with a strange man... make sure to get his license plate number! And kids, remind Mom and Dad of your old pal Officer Joe when they write out that generous check to the Police Boys Association, making America's tomorrow a little safer today!
BUDDY. Boy, I'm gonna tell my dad to make sure to—
ANNOUNCER. *(V.O.)* We interrupt this broadcast for an exclusive special news bulletin. Tragedy has struck at Mintsingue Manor, long considered by local civic groups to be an anachronistic blight on this modern suburban development. Marius Mintsingue, eccentric host of the local late night kiddie horror show, the so-called *Fear Theatre,* appearing only moments ago on this very station, has met a terrible fate. For years, Mintsingue has been entertaining his youthful fans by staging macabre scenes of self-torture and execution. This time, however, it seems the joke was on Mintsingue, when one of his patently theatrical stunts backfired. It appears that a gimmicked iron maiden didn't gimmick according to plan, and the razor-sharp spikes made mincemeat out of Mintsingue. I guess his dozens of dedicated fans can say that they saw

Mintsingue die live! We return you to regular programming. *(Pause.)* Ha! How's that for an exclusive? See what those bastards over at NBC think of me now. We're still on? FUCK!!

(BLACKOUT)

Scene 2

(Lights up almost immediately on Mintsingue Manor, which we now see in its entirety. It is Saturday afternoon. The coffin stands closed, facing upstage. GLORY HOLDEN in a blonde beehive wig and harem pants, absently leads OFFICER JOE in from the kitchen. JOE carries a notepad, although the act of writing notes seems almost too complex for him.)

GLORY. And, uh, this is the sittin' room. But you seen it already.

JOE. Nice spread.

GLORY. Used to be.

(GLORY goes to bar, begins mixing a drink.)

JOE. So who gets the joint?

GLORY. What am I, his lawyer? How should I know?

JOE. Hmph. How'd he pay for it? Not from that stupid TV show.

GLORY. Degrading, I know. But Crimestopper's Notebook was taken.

JOE. Well, I don't got money. *(Gesturing around house.)* Everything I got, I earned myself.

GLORY. *(Looks around.)* The manor was his family's. They came here in 1492, give or take. I can picture him as a five-year-old, running around the halls in ringlets and a pinafore, like Little Lady Fauntleroy.

JOE. And he was the end of the line.

GLORY. What gave you that idea? Drink?

JOE. Never on duty.

GLORY. Course. Mind if I do?

JOE. Help yourself.

GLORY. Thanks *(JOE tries closet door. Locked.)* Closet.

JOE. So, guy with a nice spread like this kicks the bucket and no family.

GLORY. *I'm* his family.

(Pause.)

JOE. Right. When did you come into the picture?

GLORY. Twenty years ago. I was just a wee slip of a girl then.

JOE. *(Bemused.)* All right... so... were there any... previous... attempts?

GLORY. On what? My honor?

JOE. Suicide...

GLORY. Suicide? Were there any suicide attempts?

JOE. All right, was he depressed?

GLORY. Vincent Price backed out of a movie and Marius was gonna take his place. He was about to get his first big break in pictures. What about that would you find depressing?

JOE. Look, let's get this over with.

GLORY. Oh, I get it. You wanna wrap this up, so it's suicide.

JOE. You got a problem with that?

GLORY. No, I think it's a great idea! No press.

JOE. Exactly.

GLORY. They shoulda brought you in on the Lindbergh baby. I bet that was a suicide too.

JOE. 'Course if your boyfriend did knock himself off, you wouldn't get any insurance dough, now wouldja?

GLORY. Listen, Officer I.Q., this ain't about insurance! The man did not—

JOE. (Interrupting.) On the other hand, you'd be surprised how many people would go to the trouble of killin' a man for his insurance. Tell you what. I want this over with fast. If I need a suspect, I'll take whoever's handy. Get me?

(Silence.)

GLORY. Depressed. He was depressed. I never seen no one so depressed.

JOE. And you say there were other attempts?

GLORY. "There were other attempts."

JOE. No. I mean, you say there were other suicide attempts.

GLORY. Oh. Yeah. Lots. Fridays, mostly.

JOE. And he didn't leave no note?

GLORY. No. Unless you need one.

JOE. No, that's all right. That's about all I need. I'll be back, but not for the stiff. You can have the undertaker pick it up.

GLORY. No, that's all right.

JOE. You're not gonna bury him in that, are ya?

GLORY. It was his favorite.

(GLORY freshens her drink. A knock at the door.)

JOE. Want me to get that?
GLORY. Wouldja? I'm "depressed."

(JOE lets in FATHER PAT. The door remains open.)

JOE. Padre! Why if it ain't good ol' Father Pat, come to save your soul.
GLORY. I'm kinda spent. Could ya do Marius first?

(GLORY turns away.)

PAT. I don't believe I've had the pleasure.

(GLORY gives a start at the sound of PAT'S voice.)

GLORY. Haven't ya?
JOE. Oh. Where's me manners? Father Pat, this is, uh, Glory Holden. The stiff's... roommate.
PAT. Surprising our never meeting before.
GLORY. Surprising.
JOE. Wasn't that nice of Father Pat to come all the way over here to administer last rites for your little friend?
GLORY. Marius wasn't a Catholic.
PAT. Oh, no?

(JOE shoots GLORY a look.)

GLORY. But he was thinkin' about it.

PAT. *(Cheered.)* Well, was he now?

GLORY. Yeah. He was sayin' "Maybe I should become a Catholic. Then I wouldn't be so depressed."

JOE. There ya go, Padre. He was depressed 'cause he wasn't Catholic!

PAT. Well, it's a little late, but I'll see what I can do.

(PAT and JOE struggle to open the iron maiden's heavy lid. It opens facing upstage.)

PAT. It's empty!

JOE. In the lid, Padre.

PAT. Oh. Well, what do ya know? Five spikes. There's a sermon in that!

JOE. Coulda been worse.

GLORY. How?

JOE. Well, for example, he coulda been burnt to death in a gasoline tank explosion.

PAT. Or nailed to a cross!

JOE. Or blown to pieces when he sat on a toilet booby-trapped with a pipe-bomb!

PAT. Or shot full of arrows, like Saint Sebastian!

JOE. Or, he coulda been stuck in the refrigerator compartment of a ship that sank to the bottom of the sea; he's struggling to get out, he's just about to suffocate, finally he pries the door open--JUST enough so the ocean comes flooding in on him, and then he drowns, his hungry lungs choking to death on salt water!

GLORY. Okay, okay, it coulda been worse! He should be grateful. *(To MINTSINGUE'S corpse:)* You should be grateful!

(PAT starts mumbling in Latin, JOE looks on, hat in hand, GLORY broods and drinks. MARTY and EDDIE stick their heads in window. GLORY waves them away, gesturing to JOE. ARNGE enters through the open front door, wearing a trenchcoat and fedora.)

ARNGE. Is this the home of Marius Mintsingue?

GLORY. Yeah, but you just missed him.

ARNGE. Buck Arnge, Federal Bureau of Investigation.

JOE. Feds!

(JOE puts on his hat.)

GLORY. More authority. I feel so safe.

ARNGE. *(Looks around.)* I was expecting something... more.

JOE. *(Saluting.)* Pleased to meet you, sir. It's a simple suicide, sir. Open and shut case.

ARNGE. Name.

JOE. What, mine? *(ARNGE glares at JOE.)* Officer Joe McCarthy, in charge of the case.

ARNGE. You were.

JOE. *(Crestfallen.)* But...

ARNGE. Suicide on the waves is a federal crime, Officer. If this man weren't dead, he'd be in serious trouble.

GLORY. *(Looking at MINTSINGUE.)* Yeah, look at him. He's smug. He's not gonna repent.

ARNGE. Where were you at the time of death, Officer Joe?

JOE. Me? What are you talking about? I'm an officer of the law!

GLORY. Yeah. That almost *makes* him innocent.

ARNGE. I'm afraid this is out of your jurisdiction, Officer. *(Turning to GLORY.)* You--what's your name?

GLORY. Glory Holden.

ARNGE. Relationship to deceased?

GLORY. *Ex*-roommate.

ARNGE. I see. *(To FATHER PAT, who is in the middle of last rites.)* You're the priest, right? Right. *(Looking around.)* That's a beautiful chaise longue. Seventeenth century?

GLORY. Well, Marius bought it new, so who knows?

ARNGE. And the house?

GLORY. Been in his family since it was fashionable. Can't you guys get together and compare notes? I hate to go through this again.

JOE. Don't mouth off to the F.B.I. Ya insult the F.B.I., you insult the good name of J. Edgar Hoover.

GLORY. Fellas, I been up all night. Gimme a break, huh?

ARNGE. No, Officer, Miss Holden's right. And I'd like to oblige. But I got this little man inside of me that tells me something doesn't sit right. *(To GLORY.)* You ever have a little man inside of ya?

GLORY. Is that a trick question?

ARNGE. No. *(To JOE.)* Officer, Miss Holden doesn't seem to appreciate the gravity of her situation. Perhaps as an officer of the law you can help cultivate her appreciative skills.

JOE. Huh? Oh. Oh, yeah!!

(JOE slaps the drink out of GLORY'S hand.)

GLORY. Hey!

(JOE slaps GLORY across the face several times, and grabs

her, twisting her arm behind her back. GLORY barely suppresses her rage.)

JOE. Listen, sister--you better make nice for the nice G-Man here, or you're gonna find that the police ain't always your friends.

ARNGE. When did you move into the manor?

GLORY. His mother left him the joint ten years ago when she kicked the bucket. We figured we'd leave the city and come out to bucolic Long Island, get some peace and quiet for a change.

ARNGE. When did you become... "friends"?

GLORY. *(In pain from JOE'S restraint.)* Twenty years. Christ!

ARNGE. What did you do before you met him?

(PAT notices fracas.)

PAT. Well, it looks as though my work here is done.

(JOE releases GLORY and neatens himself.)

JOE. Leavin' already, Padre?

PAT. The good lord's work waits for no man. I'm coachin' basketball today at the boy's club, don't ya know.

JOE. Give 'em Hell, Padre.

GLORY. Father, please stay. Please.

PAT. Why, Miss Holden. I didn't know you ta have an interest in heavenly matters.

GLORY. Interest? I can hardly wait for 'em.

PAT. Well, I have to be getting back, but perhaps I could stop by later and see what I can do to save you from eternal damnation.

JOE. Thank the nice Padre.

GLORY. Gee, thanks Father. But don't make it too much later.

PAT. *(Aside to GLORY.)* Perhaps we can get to know each other better.

ARNGE. *(To GLORY.)* You mind showing me the grounds, ma'am?

GLORY. Not at all. I was waiting for the next tour. *(To PAT and JOE.)* I'm sure I can trust you two alone. *(Leading ARNGE into the kitchen.)* And this is the kitchen. We call it that on account o' the sink.

JOE. What do you make of all this, Padre?

PAT. Sure and I'm no detective and it's not my place to judge...

JOE. Course...

PAT. And if heathens want to engage in acts against Nature, it's of no concern to me...

JOE. Couldn't of said it better...

PAT. If they want to dress up in their pagan costumes and paint their faces like harlots for their debauchery, glistening groups of them in heaps of pounding pulsating flesh, sweating and panting in one great throbbing mass...

(BUDDY and BOB appear in front doorway, a paperback of "Swann in Love" noticeably protruding from BOB'S back pocket.)

JOE. *(Aroused.)* Wow!

PAT. If they want to thrust into the hot steamy depths, writhing and reveling in the moist pockets of the nether regions... *(He notices the boys, tries to calm down.)* Well, one cheek washes the other, as the Lord sayeth.

JOE. *(Mopping his brow.)* Gee, Padre. You sure can cut up a piece of Scripture.

PAT. If you need me, I'll be at the rectory. Lads.

(PAT exits, flushed.)

JOE. Well, hello boys! What seems to be the trouble?

BOB. Well, it's Mr. Mintsingue.

JOE. No trouble there--he's dead!

(JOE points to coffin, which boys see for the first time.)

BOB. Gosh!

BUDDY. Well, heck, we know that! It's all over the radio.

JOE. Well, then, what's the problem?

BOB. The thing of it is--we think he was mysteriously murdered!!

JOE. Murdered?! We-he-hell...

BOB. That scream sure was different from how he usually screams.

BUDDY. Yeah. Scary, but not as good.

BOB. He knew the spikes were gonna close on him, so there must have been a secret escape hatch.

BUDDY. We think maybe they set it up.wrong.

BOB. Maybe they did it on purpose!

(Pause.)

BUDDY. But it couldn't have been a lone gunman because the entry wounds were from at least two different angles, and people heard gunshots from the grassy knoll *and* the book deposit... tory...

(BOB and JOE stare at BUDDY a moment.)

JOE. Well now, boys. Murder. That's a pretty serious charge.

BOB. We think so.

JOE. Sure appreciate your help, but don't you think that the police know what we're doing?

BOB. But it just doesn't add up. He hangs himself, and stabs himself, and chokes himself, and gui<u>ll</u>otines and drowns himself all the time!

BUDDY. Every time there's a commercial!

BOB. And nothing ever went wrong.

BUDDY. Yeah, and they said there wasn't gonna be an investigation. And that's no fair if it's murder!

JOE. Now, boys, don't you think that if there was any question at all, any shadow of a doubt as to whether this Mintsingue guy was the victim of anything but an accidental--though horribly bloody and no doubt, slow, torturous, and agonizing death, the police force of this town would hesitate for a moment to track down every last clue?

BUDDY. Well, no...

BOB. We just...

JOE. *(Indignant.)* We got better things to do than snoop around after some Caspar Milquetoast who swishes through town in broad daylight wearin' a cape, some sissymary you can't tell from a girl without a scorecard, some fruitcake whose very being violates the most basic tenets of God and man... *(GLORY and ARNGE re-enter. JOE continues, desperately.)* I mean, look at it from my perspective. I put in a long day. I have important things to do. I can't go around answering calls from every pansy who claims he got killed!! *(He looks around. No response. JOE is frothing.)* What's the matter with you people? Doesn't anyone trust the police?

ARNGE. Officer Joe...

JOE. *(Muttering.)* ... the badge is a badge of honor...

ARNGE. Officer Joe. Why don't you take the sarcophagus down to the station?

JOE. *(Dissipated.)* What, me?

ARNGE. Please.

JOE. By myself?

ARNGE. I think so.

(ALL watch JOE struggle to get the iron maiden through the door.)

ARNGE. And what—

(We hear the inevitable crash of the iron maiden hitting the ground. JOE peeks in.)

JOE. Sorry.

(JOE exits.)

ARNGE. And what can I do for you boys?

BUDDY. We were... just...

BOB. Helping.

BUDDY. ... helping. We came to...

BOB. Help.

BUDDY. Help.

BOB. Officer Joe.
BUDDY. Help Officer Joe.
BOB. We'll go help Officer Joe.

(Beat. BUDDY and BOB begin to run out.)

GLORY. Boys, boys., No reason to run off. These little tykes are friends of mine. Good-hearted neighborhood kids come to help out around the house. Surely the nice G-Man can spare them to good old Glory Holden, to comfort her in her hour of grief.
BUDDY. Sure!

(BOB elbows BUDDY.)

BOB. No, we better be going. Thanks, though.
ARNGE. No, that's okay, boys. I have to go question the TV announcer. The man sure had a lot of friends.
GLORY. Today he does.
ARNGE. And before this? *(No response.)* That's all I need here. You've been very helpful. *(No response. He nods to GLORY.)* Miss Holden.

(ARNGE moves to exit. PIG runs in, breathless.)

PIG. Glory, there's heat all around the—

(PIG sees ARNGE and stops dead, trying to act casual.)

GLORY. Allow me to introduce my... camera coordinator, Pig Marrano. Pig, this is Buck Arnge, Federal Bureau of Investigation.

ARNGE. Mr. Marrano.
PIG. Fed--hey, that's F.B.I.!

(ARNGE tries to stare PIG down.)

ARNGE. That's right. And we always get our man.

(ARNGE exits.)

BUDDY. Isn't that the motto of the Canadian Mounties?
GLORY. I thought I made it up. *(To BUDDY and BOB.)*
All right, you pantywaists. Whattayou want wit my house?
(To PIG.) Looka dis. More adulatin' fans.
PIG. Whaddaya wawmeda do widdem?
GLORY. Hmph! Toss 'em on the divan.

*(PIG tosses BUDDY and BOB across the room, onto the couch.
Banging comes from inside the closet door.)*

GLORY. *(To PIG.)* Did you hear anyone say "All Clear"? *I*
didn't hear anyone say "All Clear."
PIG. Should I...?
GLORY. *(Looks at kids.)* Why not? Who they gonna tell?
(PIG goes toward the closet door.) But it's been twelve hours--
you better have the net ready.

*(PIG unlocks closet door. The door slams open to reveal a
dashingly handsome man, Ronald Coleman, in evening
clothes, pencil mustache, hair brilliantined, striking a pose
in magnificent profile in the door frame.)*

ZARAH. *(MALE.)* You can imprison me, flail me with your brutal words, rob me of my last vestige of dignity, but there's one thing you can't take away: my will to live.

GLORY. It's worse than I thought.

ZARAH. *(MALE.)* The ignominy of domestic confinement was almost more than I could bear. Again and again I asked myself, "When will they leave? When? When?!"

GLORY. Sorry I couldn't work things to fit your schedule. I had more than my share of trouble explaining me without explaining you. Like I didn't have enough headaches already. Now I got two little snotnose brats sneaking around the house and tramplin' my gardenias. Whaddayiz want, ya sexless little vermin? Books? Not a chance. Souvenirs? Forget it--I burnt the lingerie collection this morning. *(ZARAH sighs.)* He was in tears, believe you me. Well, half in tears, anyways.

PIG. The cop took Marius!

GLORY. That ain't the half of it. *(Pacing.)* First someone ventilates the man who watched me get beached on the sands of time. Then the local heat grills me all night, but the fed thinks I'm not done yet. So he teams up with the local to play tag-team proctologists on me.

ZARAH. *(MALE.)* Marius would've known what to do. Somehow he always knew what to do.

GLORY. Great. Why don't you go ask him?

ZARAH. *(MALE.)* My dear lady, I simply meant...

GLORY. The queen is dead. No offense to the Brains Trust over here, but if anybody's gonna know what to do now, it's me.

(Long pause. ZARAH and PIG look to GLORY expectantly. GLORY notices them.)

GLORY. What?

BOB. So this is Mintsingue Manor.

BUDDY. Except for how scary it looks on the outside, this is kind of a nice place.

BOB. Yeah. Just the opposite of my house.

GLORY. Is that so? Pig, bring these two insects some tea and lady fingers! *(PIG exits to kitchen.)* Can you believe the cop with that line about suicide?! Suicide my left tit! It was straight outta *Stage Door*--Vincent Price is making his latest flick, *Palace of Plasma*. He's havin' a boys'-night-out with Charles Laughton, twists his ankle on the dance floor, he can't go on. They gotta find somebody right away--old family, classical training, but every bit as masculine as Vinnie. And who do they pick? Marius Makepeace Minsingue. *(PIG enters with tea and ladyfingers.)* His big break, the one he waited for all his life. Now he's finally gonna make pictures. So *then* he goes out and pulls a Saint Sebastian on himself? Tell it to the tykes who watched that goofy show! Maybe they'll believe it!

BUDDY. Whaddaya mean, "goofy"?

PIG. I can't understand it. We rehearsed it a dozen times. The back panel opens the second he hits the button. I catch him, the door closes, he screams, we cut to credits.

ZARAH. *(MALE.)* Gentle bard, cut down in your prime. Would that the savage swine who swilled the precious nectar of your art had only gazed upon the diamond in their midst. Perhaps I was the only one who could truly understand him, as he alone understood me.

PIG. Don't get soft on me now. You gotta be strong.

(As ZARAH speaks, she turns to show the audience the side appropriate to the gender in which she is speaking.)

ZARAH. *(MALE.)* Don't tell me that. It's always been like that: "Calm down." "Stop acting like a girl." *(FEMALE.)* Well, I am a girl--*(MALE.)* sometimes. *(FEMALE.)* And sometimes I'm a man. A very manly man. With a man's needs, a man's wants, a man's desires. Then suddenly it hits me: *(MALE, showing both sides.)* I'm a woman!

GLORY. Anybody got some Dramamine?--I'm gettin' motion sickness.

BUDDY. I always put my head between my legs.

(GLORY stares at him.)

ZARAH. *(FEMALE.)* I tried to go about as a woman, fully a woman, but I couldn't suppress my manly desires. I like to have a beer with ze boys. I like to watch ze fights. I like to hang out at ze construction site and whistle at ze babes while adjusting my baskette. It's all so simple, *(MALE.)* and all so terribly terribly strange. When my twin sister died, a part of me died too. I felt somehow *(struggling for words. FEMALE.)* ...torn asunder, *(MALE.)* ... cleft in twain...

GLORY. Bi-sected?

ZARAH. *(MALE.)* If you will. I was all alone, ready to end it all. That was when I met Marius. *(FEMALE.)* He took me in among you lovely people, got me a job at Hubert's Museum of Human Oddities--*(MALE.)* Nothing glamorous, but it was stable, and I didn't have to hide who I was. *(FEMALE.)* He promised to take me into the movies once he got his big break. But it was not to be. *(MALE.)* Don't you all see? It simply can't have been suicide. *(FEMALE.)* A great beacon would not snuff out its own flame.

(ZARAH sobs.)

PIG. Now, don't go off half-cocked!

GLORY. Yeah, you're beside yourself.

PIG. All's I wanna know is, when do we get the insurance dough?

GLORY. We don't.

PIG. What do you mean?

GLORY. If we so much as start sniffing around them shekels, I'll have the whole police force marching up my lower intestine. We gotta—

ZARAH. *(FEMALE.)* Oh, money money money. A great artiste has died. Who can think about money at a time like this?!

GLORY. Yeah, you're right. We can all get real jobs based on our marketable skills. Pig can shake down paperboys, and I can collect deposit bottles. But what can *you* do?

PIG. What about his estate?

GLORY. You're sittin' in it. *(Gestures to the house.)* The Mintsingue Family legacy. And if the roof don't leak, we can stay dry all winter. We couldn't even get through the month if we didn't get that advance on the *(glances at BUDDY and BOB)* you-know-what from the Verbissene *(pronounced "fer-BISS-uh-nuh")* brothers. *(PIG and ZARAH exchange worried looks.)* Don't tell me.

PIG. She needed a new outfit. For the you-know-what!

GLORY. All of it?!

PIG. Aw, you know, accessories...

GLORY. Pig!!

ZARAH. *(FEMALE.)* Money money money money...!

GLORY. They want to pick up the you-know-what tomorrow

morning. Before church. Now we can't even give 'em the money back!

BUDDY. *(Mouth full of ladyfingers.)* Hey, what's a "you-know-what"?

GLORY. What're you two twinkies still doing in my house? Cantcha see I'm grieving over here?

(BUDDY and BOB exchange looks, and begin to leave.)

BUDDY. Hey, can I ask you one question? *(Points to PIG and GLORY.)* How come only you and you were in the papers? They didn't mention anyone else.

GLORY. My friend is camera shy. What's it to you?

BUDDY. Oh, nothin'. I was just...

BOB. We just came by for souvenirs, like you said.

PIG. She told ya. She burned everything!

GLORY. Sh! Yeah, it's like my friend says, there ain't nothin' left.

BUDDY. Wow! You must've been really upset!

BOB. Sh!

PIG. *(To BUDDY.)* Whaddaya mean by that?

GLORY. *(To PIG.)* Sh! *(To BUDDY.)* Whaddaya mean by that?

BOB. He means if you burned everything like you said. His costumes, his pictures, his...

GLORY. *(Overlapping.)* Everything!

BOB. ... books.

GLORY. *(Pause.)* Who sent you boys here?

BUDDY. *(Cheerfully.)* Nobody. We just came here on our own. Bob said if...

GLORY. Nobody?

BUDDY. Nope!
BOB. It's true.
PIG. And nobody knows you're here?
BOB. Not a soul.

*(GLORY and PIG exchange looks. PIG takes ZARAH upstairs,
ZARAH noticing BOB as she passes. GLORY regards BOB.)*

GLORY. Say, kid--are you by any chance... artistic?
BOB. *(Nervous.)* What do you m—
BUDDY. *(Interrupting.) Is he?!* Boy, you said a mouthful!
Bob's the best artist of anybody--seventh, eighth, *or* ninth!
You oughta see him draw superheroes! His room--he has one
wall, the whole wall, prolly a *thousand* pictures of Superman!
He even did one of him changing into his costume, and they
never show that in the com—
BOB. *(Interrupting.)* Buddy!!
GLORY. Don't sweat it, kid. I'm a Superman fan from way
back.
BOB. Really?
GLORY. Big time. Say, I'll betcha always thought he was
too good for that Lois Lane, huh?
BUDDY. No way! They make a great coup— *(GLORY
shoots BUDDY a look.)* —le.
BOB. *(Amazed.)* Yeah, she's always--How did *you* know?
BUDDY. Hey, doesn't anybody wanna know *my* opinion?!
GLORY. Kid, I hate to tell you this, but I knew your opin-
ion before you was born.

*(BUDDY'S face mirrors his mind's movement from conster-
nation to glee at the science-fictive aura of GLORY'S claim.)*

BUDDY. Neat!!!

BOB. Well, thanks Miste— Miss—

GLORY. Glory. *(To BUDDY.)* And you can call me Miss Holden.

BOB. Thanks, Glory. And... thanks.

BUDDY. *(Bursting.)* Hey, what am I thinking now?!

BOB. C'mon , pal. We better go home.

BUDDY. Not even close! Anyway, I was asking Miss Holden! She's the one who knows my thoughts!

GLORY. Aw, shucks, kid. It ain't much. Believe me.

BUDDY. Gosh!

(We hear a crash from upstairs.)

ZARAH. *(Off. Through Bitter Tears.)* Oh, je m'en fou!!

PIG. *(Off.)* Glory!

GLORY. *(To BUDDY and BOB.)* Now listen youse two—

(PIG peeks in from the stairwell.)

PIG. Glory, could you, uh... she's acting... you know.

(GLORY nods to PIG, who disappears up the stairs. GLORY turns to BOB.)

GLORY. Come back first thing in the morning, and I'll give you all the souvenirs you want.

ZARAH. *(Off.)* J'accuse!

GLORY. *(To BOB.)* And kid! Not a word to your officer friend about *(Nods to stairs.)* --Fred and Ginger up there. Do we have a deal? *(BOB nods.)* I hope you'll excuse me for not seeing yiz out--I gotta go take care of the French Resistance.

(GLORY exits upstairs.)

BUDDY. That Miss Holden is real nice, huh? It's awful when tragedy strikes such a nice family!

BOB. Yeah, I guess... But how about all that stuff she was saying about Marius? If he was getting his big break, he just couldn't have killed himself.

BUDDY. Gee, I thought he was already famous. We've been watching him forever.

BOB. Didn't you think she was acting suspicious about the insurance money?

BUDDY. Maybe she killed him for it.

BOB. *(Reluctantly.)* M-maybe...

BUDDY. Hey, are we having a hunch?

BOB. Yeah, I guess.

BUDDY. Aw*right*ey!

(Enter MARTY and EDDIE through window.)

EDDIE. Well, well, if it ain't the Hardy Boys.

MARTY. Don't you mean the Hardly Boys?

(EDDIE and MARTY laugh.)

EDDIE. Yeah, that's right--Francine and Josephine!

MARTY. Officer Joe told us down at the Boys' Club about youse two tryna solve the mystery of that fruitcake bitin' the dust.

BUDDY. He's not a fruitcake, he's cool!

MARTY. Yeah, he's real cool, alright. He's ice cold!

(MARTY and EDDIE laugh.)

BOB. That's not funny.

MARTY. Naw, maybe it ain't. Maybe it's you two who's a little funny, if you know what I mean.

BUDDY. What do you mean?

MARTY. Maybe we oughta call you Hardly Boys the *Hard-Up Boys* instead!

EDDIE. Yeah, that's right! When's the last time one of you sissy-boys had a date, huh?

MARTY. What're you talkin' about, Eddie? They have plenty of dates.

EDDIE. Oh, yeah?

MARTY. Yeah, they're havin' a date right now--with each other!

BUDDY. (Indignant.) No we're not! We're boys!

MARTY. Now don't be shy, pipsqueak. How's about showin' us a little romantic kiss?

(MARTY tries to push BUDDY'S and BOB'S heads together. BUDDY pushes away.)

BUDDY. Cut it out, you bully!

EDDIE. Aw, shuddup, squirt. Your mutha sells potato chips.

BUDDY. No she doesn't!

EDDIE. Oh yeah? How come I seen her goin' down the street the other day, yellin' "Lays--fi' cents!!"?

(MARTY and EDDIE laugh.)

BUDDY. My mom does *not* sell potato chips!

BOB. C'mon, Buddy. Let's go.

BUDDY. Maybe *your* mother sells potato chips...

EDDIE. *(Nose-to-nose with BUDDY.)* My mutha... is dead.

BUDDY. Oh. Sorry.

EDDIE. Yeah, right.

BUDDY. But maybe she used to sell potato chips!

EDDIE. My mother did *not*--Look, shrimpboat, this is not about potato chips!

BUDDY. OH, sure--you're just saying that now 'cause you don't really *know* if she sold 'em or not!

EDDIE. I don't bel*ieve* this little runt...!

BOB. C'mon, Buddy, let's get outta here.

MARTY. Hey, hey, Sherlock--where you goin'? I wanna talk to you some more.

BOB. Wh-wh-whattaya want?

(EDDIE and MARTY surround BUDDY and BOB.)

MARTY. Hey, uh, who's your favorite singer--Perry Homo?

MARTY and EDDIE. Perry Homo! Ha, ha, ha!

EDDIE. Yeah, yeah, an' what's your favorite song--"Homo on the Range"?

MARTY and EDDIE. "Homo on the Range"! That's a good one! Ha, ha, ha! Oh, dat's rich!

BOB. Maybe you fellas are homos, but not us.

BUDDY. Yeah, we don't wear girls' dresses and make-up and stuff like that!

MARTY. Hey, hey, wait a secint. Did I hear you right?

BOB. What?

BUDDY. Yeah, what?

MARTY. You just called us homos.

BOB. No I didn't.

MARTY. Yeah, you did. You just said "We're not homos, you guys are homos."

BUDDY. No, he said maybe you guys were, but we're not. It wasn't a naive contention of objective reality but rather a contemplation of the range of ontological possibility, as if to say "It's theoretically conceivable that—"

(BUDDY chokes as EDDIE lifts him by the collar.)

EDDIE. You know what Marty did to the last guy who called him a homo?

BUDDY. *(Choking.)* Poked holes in the faulty logic of his arguments?

MARTY. I made him cop my joint.

BOB. Cop your joint?

MARTY. You know, suckle my kielbasa.

BUDDY. Suckle your kielbasa?

MARTY. *(Increasingly frustrated.)* I made him play a tune on my skin flute.

BUDDY and BOB. Play a tune on your skin flute?!

MARTY. OH, for crying out loud! I made him suck my dick, okay?!

BUDDY and BOB. Ohhhh!

BUDDY. What?

EDDIE. Yeah. You showed him, Marty. He'll never call you a homo again.

MARTY. Yeah, I messed him up for good. But you two are just a couple o' little wieners. So I'm just gonna beat the shit outta ya. Whaddaya say, Eddie?

EDDIE. Yeah, okay.

(BUDDY and BOB are beaten viciously and realistically, long enough that the audience will be disturbed. MARTY and EDDIE exit to kitchen.)

BUDDY. Bob? You okay?

(Silence. Then BOB sobs for a few moments. ZARAH enters from the stairs, looking refreshed, singing "La Vie en Rose.")

ZARAH. Oh! Mes pauvres bébés! What happened to vous!
BUDDY. Those bad kids beat us up.
ZARAH. *(To BUDDY.)* OH! Quelle damage! *(She shoves BUDDY aside and cradles BOB in her arms.)* Oh, mon soldier de courage, what have they done to you?
BOB. *(Sniffling.)* They--they hit me in the mouth, and the eye, and the back, and the... stomach...
BUDDY. Really hard!
BOB. And then they picked up Buddy and started hitting me with him.
BUDDY. Yeah. Like this.

(BUDDY demonstrates, pounding his head against BOB.)

ZARAH. Non! Maman will fix you up! *(Offhand to BUDDY.)* And you too. *(She goes to bar, returns with two wet cloths, throws one at BUDDY, begins wiping BOB'S face with the other.)* How does that eye feel?
BOB. Hurts.
BUDDY. Mine hurts a lot!

BOB. Thanks for being so nice.

ZARAH. Mais oui! Those nasty bullies. Their words torment us, their fists beat us. Some of the scars fade, some never go away. If I had been here *(Suddenly MALE and furious.)* I'd've rent them calf from crown. I'd've made short shrift of them, mark my words! I'd... *(FEMALE.)* Oh! I forget myself!

BOB. *(To BUDDY.)* Maybe this wasn't such a good idea after all.

BUDDY. But we're just getting started. Besides, detectives get beat up all the time.

BOB. Buddy!

ZARAH. Detectives? Oh, Maman understands. You are after a murderer?

(BOB glares at BUDDY.)

BOB. Well, sort of.

BUDDY. Mr. Mintsingue's girlfriend sure was upset about that insurance money...

ZARAH. *(MALE.)* Surely you're not suggesting she killed him for it?

BOB. Well, we don't know...

ZARAH. *(FEMALE.)* Ah.

BUDDY. Where were you the night Mr. Mintsingue was murdered?

BOB. Buddy!

ZARAH. No, it's all right. I was not here.

BUDDY. Oh. Well, that lets you out.

BOB. Do you have an alibi?

ZARAH. *(Eyes tearing.)* Non.

BOB. Well, you know what people will think.

ZARAH. *(Breaking down.)* I know what zey'll think. And it's twue. It's twue.

(BOB grabs ZARAH by the shoulders.)

BOB. But do you realize what this means? If they find out, it's all over for you!

ZARAH. *(Through tears.)* Oh, it's all over already! *(She sobs on BOB'S shoulder. Insistent knocking at front door.)* You must help me!

BOB. I'll help you. Go! Hide!

(ZARAH goes to stairs.)

ZARAH. And Maman will not forget you!

(ZARAH ascends stairs.)

BUDDY. Wow! You sure are a great detective!

BOB. Buddy, what if somebody finds out—

BUDDY. I mean it! You could be a private eye in real life!

(Front door opens and OFFICER JOE sticks his head in.)

BUDDY. Officer Joe!

BOB. We were just leaving. Honest.!

JOE. That G-Man still snooping around here?

BUDDY. Uh...

JOE. *(Enters, pacing.)* What is it with that guy, muscling in on my beat. I had this case wrapped up, open and shut. Now I'm gonna prove this was suicide, even if I have to find evidence to do it!

BUDDY. *(Very excited.)* Evidence! We have great evidence!

BOB. Buddy!

BUDDY. And it wasn't Miss Holden!

JOE. Miss Hol--? This isn't about murder again, is it?

BUDDY. Yeah, and it couldn't have been Miss Holden, right, Bob?

JOE. *(To BOB.)* Well, Mr. Junior G-Man, if you're so sure it was a murder, who *did* do it, then?

BOB. Well, it's kinda confusing.

JOE. Tell you what, kid--don't waste your money on badge polish. I didn't get to be the star of "Crimestopper's Notebook" by takin' potshot guesses like some amateur.

(Enter MARTY and EDDIE from kitchen.)

MARTY. *(Low.)* Look, it's the Hardy Girls with Officer Joe. *(Normal.)* Hey, Officer Joe! We was just talkin' about you.

EDDIE. Yeah, we was just sayin' we wanna be cops when we grow up.

MARTY. Yeah, you guys got it made.

JOE. *(Cheered.)* Why, that's swell, fellas. The force is made up of guys just like you. Guys who know the difference between right and wrong, and what it's worth.

BUDDY. Hey, those guys beat us up!

EDDIE. Ah, quit cryin'!

MARTY. What're ya, a baby?

BUDDY. You did too, you big creeps!

JOE. We-heh-hell, I guess I can't see the harm in a little roughhousing now and then. It keeps up the ol' reflexes. And it's a real morale booster.

BUDDY. But—

JOE. Buddy, when two young fellas duke it out, there's only one outcome: a winner, and a loser. Now if you make the mistake of being the loser, why, next time you just have to go in there and hit 'em twice as hard! Then you'll be the winner!

MARTY. That's a great idea, Officer Joe--we're gonna go down to the Boys' Club and get some sparring practice right now!

JOE. Knock 'em dead, boys.

(MARTY pats BOB on the shoulder.)

MARTY. See y'around, chum. *(FATHER PAT enters with flowers, surprised at the crowd. Ditches flowers.)* Hey, Fodda Pat! Whaddaya hear, whaddaya say?

FATHER PAT. Oh! Hello, lads. I bet you're all wonderin' what I'm doing here.

MARTY. No.

EDDIE. Hey, Padre. We're headed over to the Boys Club to keep outta trouble, just like you're always sayin'.

MARTY. Yeah, we're gonna find a healthy outlet for our aggressions so's we don't hafta inflict our own inner conflicts on people who bear us no ill will. If you know what I mean.

FATHER PAT. Why, that's fine, boys, just fine. And remember, if your muscles feel sore after a good manly pounding—

MARTY. Yeah, we know. Your office is right next to the locker room. Later, Padre. *(To EDDIE:)* Or is it "Madre"?

(MARTY and EDDIE laugh, exit front door.)

FATHER PAT. Well, if it isn't young Anderson and Brady, with fine young Officer Joe, protectin' and servin' as always!

OFFICER JOE. I do my part.

FATHER PAT. There's a saying in the world of the theatre, "I'd do anything for that part."

BUDDY. Gee, Father Pat! You don't think they mean that, do you?

FATHER PAT. Sure and it's just a figure o' speech. Thespians are every bit as moral as the clergy.

OFFICER JOE. I've always had kind of a fantasy about thespians. It starts with me walkin' the beat, looking in the windows to make sure all's well, just like I always do. I look in one window and what do I see but *two* thespians, face to face, kissing. Next thing I know they're on the bed, tearing each other's clothes off, and that's all I can stand--I throw open the window and climb in. First they scream, but once I strip down to my birthday suit and they see this stunning specimen of red-white-and-blue American manhood, they're all over me like white on rice. I tell one of 'em--the blonde--to get on top of her friend, nosey-toesy, and—

FATHER PAT. Officer Joseph! You're forgetting yourself!

OFFICER JOE. Forgetting myself? I was just about to feed my nightstick to the redhead when you--*(Realizing where he is.)* Holy shit!

FATHER PAT. These lads surely wouldn't understand your allegory for the blandishments of the life of crime.

OFFICER JOE. My...? Oh. Yeah. My allergy. Well...

FATHER PAT. Boys, what young Officer Joe was trying to demonstrate by that little fable is that temptation, the temptations of womanflesh, can be strong, strong indeed, but we must be stronger. We must stand strong in the storm, like Odysseus lashed to the mast, strong against the siren-songs of the wily woman who would use us for her own invidious needs. We must cherish our fellow men, and remember that our first allegiance is always to them.

BOB. *(Sotto voce.)* Look, Officer Joe, I know it looks suspicious and everything, but I really don't think it was suicide, and I don't think it was Miss Holden, either. I think someone's trying to set her up or something.

JOE. Now, son, these people are killing themselves off all the time. Not a day goes by we don't find one of 'em cut to ribbons in the park, or floating belly-up off a pier, or brained in some men's room somewheres. It's part of their... lifestyle. Who are we to question?

FATHER PAT. *(Nervously.)* Heh-heh. Officer Joe's right, boys. Some things are better left unknown. It's like lookin' in a well--lookin's fine, but look too deep, and you might fall in.

BOB. But--but--isn't the truth important?

BUDDY. Yeah, isn't it?

(PAT and JOE look at each other, burst into laughter. They get up to leave.)

JOE. *(Shaking his head.)* Kids!

FATHER PAT. So long lads. Don't forget Mass tomorrow, Buddy. And remember, the both of you--the Lord helps those who don't question glass houses!

(PAT and JOE exit.)

BUDDY. *(Steamed.)* Ooh, if only people realized it wasn't just a kids show, they'd wanna know what really happened.

BOB. Y'know, Bud, maybe that's not it. Maybe that's not it at all.

PIG. *(Off.)* Zarah, don't!

(BUDDY and BOB hide behind bar.)

ZARAH. *(Off, MALE.)* Leave me be! I shan't be restrained!

(BUDDY peeks above bar.)

BUDDY. Does this mean we're onto something?

(BOB pulls him down as ZARAH enters from stairs, pursued by PIG and GLORY.)

GLORY. Jesus, the cop! *(GLORY looks for JOE, doesn't see him.)* Where is he?
PIG. *(Checking the door.)* He's gone. With the priest.
GLORY. *(Relieved.)* I wish them all the best.
PIG. Honey, for Christ's sake, we can't make a whole new movie in one night.

(BUDDY'S head pops up like a jack-in-the-box. BOB'S hand pulls it down.)

ZARAH. *(FEMALE.)* I have all the dialogue written. Marius told me I could say anything I wanted!
GLORY. Marius is in a file drawer in the county morgue. I'm in charge now, and ya can't add six hours of dialogue to a one-reeler!
PIG. Besides, I like the lines we say now!
GLORY. Listen, toots--I feel for ya. Honest I do. I wanted to go legit myself, once. There's nothing more humiliating for

a true actor than traipsing around a stage in some fruity costume. But this ain't your big break--it's gotta be done by morning!

ZARAH. You don't believe in me. *He* did. *(MALE.)* He said I was the greatest thing since Lunt and Fontanne.

PIG. (Pleading.) Zarah...

(A small "BOOM" is heard, and all the lights go out. The characters are silhouetted by fading daylight from the window.)

GLORY. Terrific.

(A knock at the door.)

PIG. I'll go find the fuse box.

(GLORY opens the door. A dark figure is silhouetted in the doorway.)

GLORY. Whattya wa...

(GLORY is sapped over the head. She falls to the ground with a groan. ZARAH screams. Two shots ring out, and ZARAH falls, letting out a death-scream, high and low.)

PIG. Zarah! Oh, God, Zarah!

(BLACKOUT)

END OF ACT I

ACT II

Scene 1

(The main room at Mintsingue Manor. Saturday night, well past midnight. The window is dark. GLORY is stretched out on the couch, eyes closed, a bruise on her forehead. She has not slept since Friday morning. PIG is at the bar, filling an ice bag. He takes it to her, placing it gently on her forehead. She jumps, startled.)

GLORY. Aaah!

PIG. It's just me.

GLORY. Don't sneak up on me like that.

PIG. How's that?

GLORY. Cold.

PIG. Well, yeah. It's ice.

GLORY. Those cops were a big help.

PIG. Always hasslin' ya. And when you need 'em, where are they?

GLORY. It's like my mother used to say. Never a service man around when you need one. And she needed one.

PIG. Bump still hurtin' ya?

GLORY. I'm all right. How's she?

PIG. Just a flesh wound. I patched it up okay.

GLORY. I dunno. A skull ain't too fleshy. Hers more than most, but still.

51

PIG. Well, she is acting a little loopy.

GLORY. She's always a little loopy.

PIG. No. I mean, She's Acting A Little Loopy. Anyways, she put on the hospital costume and now she's laid up in bed like Garbo.

GLORY. She comin' down?

PIG. Nah. Said she wants to be alone.

GLORY. The cops didn't see her, did they?

PIG. Unh-uh. I left her out of the story, too.

GLORY. Slick. What'd you tell them?

PIG. Some guy sapped you, fired a couple of shots, and left.

GLORY. Yeah, no big deal. Happens all the time. Specially this time of year.

PIG. Don't let it get to ya.

GLORY. Nah, I'm sure you get used to it. If you get a chance.

PIG. Hey, you're lucky. They weren't after you.

GLORY. How do you know?

PIG. You were right in the door. If they'd a wanted ya, they'd a got ya.

GLORY. So why do they want her?

PIG. Who knows? All's I know is, we gotta make sure they don't get her.

GLORY. Swell. We'll just hang out the old sign. "No actors, dogs, or murderers."

PIG. I'm way ahead a ya. I been wantin' to booby-trap this place for years, but Mister M. would never give me the go-ahead. Now if I was tryna plug somebody and I messed up the first time--which I wouldn't--the last place I'd go is through the front door, so ya gotta cover every possible point of entry in a big way: one fragmentation device, properly deployed, can blow a guy into so many pieces his own dentist won't recognize his teeth. I figure I rig a bazooka over the back stairs, trip-wire all the windows with grenades, anti-personnel mines around the whole defensive perimeter, and pukka sticks in the rose beds. Then I—

GLORY. Pukka sticks?

PIG. It's easy! I learnt it on Guam. You cut up some bamboo into pieces yea big, sharpen the edges, dip 'em in poison, and stick 'em in the mud. Guy steps on 'em--BAM!--they go right through his foot, he's dead in an hour.

GLORY. Don't forget a depth charge in the terlet.

PIG. Yeah, but what if we hafta--Oh.

GLORY. Pig, all's we're tryna do is stay alive. How's about if you just keep an eye on the doors?

PIG. (Disappointed.) Okay...

GLORY. I better make sure she's stayin' in bed. A head injury's a serious thing, even for her.

PIG. Well, she still wants to finish the movie.

GLORY. Tonight? Is she crazy?

PIG. She's right, Glory. We still gotta finish shooting by morning.

GLORY. There's cops all over the place.

PIG. Who do you wanna argue with--the cops or the Verbissene brothers?

GLORY. Gee, cement shoes or striped pajamas. Tough choice. (Pause.) I don't care. Whatever she wants. Bring her down. (PIG exits. GLORY talks to herself.) They'll show the movie at our execution. We'll be the biggest stars since Sacco and Vanzetti. (She goes to the bar, mixes a drink.) And Julius and Ethel Rosenberg. I hear they were gonna have their own TV show, but they got cancelled. Both of 'em. (Drinks.) Ah, maybe it'll be nothing that formal. Maybe the townsfolk'll just take us out and hang us. How's that for strange fruit? *(PIG re-enters in--at least--Lone Ranger mask and black socks, with a hospital screen and cot which he sets up. ZARAH enters from upstairs in hospital costume, her female side in a negligee, her male side in what may be pajamas or scrubs, with a white bandage wrapped around her head like a turban. She walks regally, but unsteadily, into a wall. GLORY covers her own face in despair.)* That wall holdin' up okay? Good.

(PIG rights ZARAH and leads her to the cot. PIG hands GLORY a small movie camera.)

PIG. Ya turn this to make it focus, this expands and con-tracts...

GLORY. Trust me--I've seen him do it a thousand times. Kill the overhead. *(PIG turns off the light. ZARAH wanders off, and PIG brings her back again. They are now lit only by a lamp or two, and are mostly in silhouette.)* Ready? Action

PIG. *(Reciting badly.)* Sorry to keep you waiting, Mr. Smith. I have many patients today. Oh, pardon me. You must be Miss Jones, here for your fertility test.

ZARAH. Zat's all right. Why don't you come in and make yourself comfortable?

PIG. I guess I will.

(Sound of unzipping.)

ZARAH. *(Before PIG gets near.)* Ohh, Marius, I....

(ZARAH sobs.)

GLORY. CUT!! *(GLORY flicks the lights on.)* Maybe we oughtta take five, while the actors prepare.

ZARAH. *(Crying.)* I'm sorry. I can't.

GLORY. Who said ya had to?

(GLORY goes for a drink.)

PIG. Yeah, doll. I'll do all the work. You just go, "Oh, oh, oh."

(PIG goes to mix drinks.)

GLORY. There's the pro.

(PIG brings drink to ZARAH.)

PIG. This acting stuff ain't so bad. I'm kinda gettin' the swing of it.

ZARAH. One minute he was alive, and now...

(ZARAH weeps.)

GLORY. You really wanna go through with this?

ZARAH. He would have wanted it this way.

GLORY. I'll give ya that. The man loved a good come shot. *(Pause.)* You ready?

ZARAH. *(Sniffling.)* I guess so.

PIG. That's the trooper!

(They take positions.)

GLORY. Now, slap some life into that thing. We're makin' art here.

PIG. Just a second. *(He slaps.)* C'mon ya lazy goldbricker! Snap to it! Ten hut!

GLORY. Pig...

PIG. Stand up straight! Suck in that gut! Ya call that military posture?!

GLORY. Pig...

PIG. Put some starch in that spine! That's the spirit! Raise that flag so everyone can see!

GLORY. Pig!

PIG. Huh?

GLORY. It was a figure of speech.

PIG. Oh.

GLORY. *(To ZARAH.)* And you--Star Quality! Ya said ya wanted to be in pictures. How's about some acting? Quiet on the set! Rolling! "A Woman's a Two-Face" take two. And... action!

PIG. *(Monotone.)* What are you? A man... or a woman?

ZARAH. *(MALE.)* Well, maybe I'm one, *(FEMALE.)* and mebbe I'm ze ozzer.

PUG. Well, let's just see if you take it like a man.

(Sound of tearing cloth.)

ZARAH. *(MALE.)* Now just a darned second! *(FEMALE.)* Oh, mon dieu! *(MALE.)* Why, if I were a man I'd *(FEMALE.)* Oh, sacre bleu! *(MALE.)* Oh! *(FEMALE.)* Oh! *(MALE.)* OH! *(FEMALE.)* OH! *(MALE.)* OHHH! *(FEMALE.)* OHHHH!!

(Doorbell rings. GLORY jumps.)

GLORY. What the—?! I bet Visconti doesn't have these problems. Take five, you lovebirds. If you can be any less mobile than you already are. Pig, cover me.

PIG. *(To ZARAH.)* Lighten up, Babe. You're blockin'.

ZARAH. I want her to be strong, yet vulnerable.

GLORY. I'm comin', I'm comin'! *(To PIG.)* Write that down-- we can use that! *(Carefully checks peephole.)* Holy Cheese, it's the Fed!

(PIG quickly covers himself, wraps ZARAH in a kimono, and tries to move her out of the room. ZARAH breaks away, and PIG collects clothing.)

ZARAH. But we hardly had time for exposition!

GLORY. I'll expose ya later. Clean this stuff up. And you keep out of sight or we're sunk.

ZARAH. It's not fair! If I have to hide, why don't you?

GLORY. I'm passing.

ZARAH. Am I not "passing"?

GLORY. Like a kidney stone. *(GLORY shoves ZARAH through kitchen door. As GLORY walks to answer door, the sound of window breaking, as stone bounces in through window. GLORY freezes. Pause. Deadpan.)* Okay. Now I'm scared.

PIG. Lemme out there, I'll chase 'em down.

GLORY. No time for that. Prolly just some kids from down the street, playing a harmless little prank. Right. *(Hands PIG the rock. Gesturing to kitchen.)* You keep her under wraps. I'll get the door.

(PIG exits to kitchen. GLORY answers the door.)

GLORY. Well, well. Top of the middle of the night to ya.

ARNGE. Sorry to bother you at this late hour, Ma'am. I noticed the lights on and thought I'd ask you a few pertinent questions.

GLORY. I was just goin' to sleep.

ARNGE. This won't take long. I've been talking with the man from Mutually Dependent Life.

GLORY. Who?

ARNGE. The late Mr. Mintsingue's insurance company. I thought you'd recognize the name.

GLORY. Mutually Dependent Life? I never heard of such a thing. *(Sultry.)* Won't you... come in?

ARNGE. That's a lovely tête-à-tête.

GLORY. Thanks.

ARNGE. Reproduction?

GLORY. *(Distracted.)* I thought about hormones once...

ARNGE. I meant the seat.

(GLORY sits on sofa, watching ARNGE. ARNGE looks at his notepad, saunters about, surveying.)

ARNGE. You seem a little piqued.

GLORY. I peaked years ago. Smoke?

ARNGE. Never on duty. *(GLORY, watching ARNGE, takes a cigar from the box on the table, and begins to light it before she realizes it is a cigar. She manages to ditch it before he looks up.)* As you know, the circumstances of Mr. Mintsingue's death were somewhat...mysterious.

GLORY. *(Aside.)* That's nothing. You shoulda seen the circumstances of his life.

ARNGE. There'll be an investigation into his past before

the insurance company can pay any claims to his beneficiaries...and I thought that might shed a little light on *our*
investigation.

GLORY. *Our* investigation?

ARNGE. To protect its investors, an insurance company
investigates every claim--to make sure it's not being defrauded.
By the beneficiaries. *(ARNGE stares GLORY down. GLORY
swallows.)* The Bureau, on the other had, always tires to put
together a comprehensive picture of a man: *(Increasingly menacing.)* who his "companions" are, where he "socializes," his
"hobbies," the nature of his close personal relationships... *(Sees
the music box, touches, perhaps picks it up.)* We feel we're
doing him a better service that way. Bisque. Very nice. *(Puts it
down.)* After all, we work for the American people.

GLORY. *(Squirming.)* Thanks.

ARNGE. Of course the companies have devised certain
rules to protect themselves. For example, Article Thirteen of
Mr. Mintsingue's own policy says that if the insured is known
to be legally insane, the policy is declared null and void. That's
what's known as the Sanity Clause.

GLORY. *(Deadpan.)* I didn't know there was a Sanity Clause.

ARNGE. Well, there is.

GLORY. But that's not fair. They knew he was an actor
when he took out the policy.

ARNGE. Now, I know this may be difficult, but was there
anything unusual about Mr. Mintsingue's habits? *(GLORY rolls
eyes.)* Anything that would indicate some, well... irregularity?

*(ZARAH appears from the kitchen, in a French maid's outfit,
with an enormous platter of phalluses and enemas. Begins
to announce.)*

ZARAH. Breakfast...

(PIG grabs ZARAH from behind and pulls her back into the kitchen. ARNGE doesn't see her.)

GLORY. Irregularity?! Why he was the most regular guy I ever met!

ARNGE. Yes, yes, I understand. But did he have any peculiar habits? Anything that might have been considered... abnormal?

GLORY. Marius Mintsingue had the most normal habits in the world. Don't listen to them rumors. He was an artist. *(ARNGE writes on pad.)* But I mean that in a nice way!

ARNGE. He certainly did some queer things on television.

GLORY. That's just show biz. It was all a fake. At home, he was nothin' but a stable family man, like you and me.

(DOORBELL rings; GLORY jumps; ZARAH appears in kitchen doorway.)

ZARAH. Do you want me to...

(PIG pulls ZARAH back into the kitchen and takes her place, clearing his throat, before ARNGE turns around.)

PIG. Do you wawmeda get that?

GLORY. Certainement! *(To ARNGE.)* You know my footman, Pig Marrano.

PIG. How ya doin'.

(PIG goes to door. GLORY rises, walks to MINSINGUE'S portrait.)

GLORY. Why, every day, regular as knockwurst, he'd come home to his family at the same time, read his paper in the family room, and sit down with the family for a nice family dinner. You'd have to go a long way to find a more stable family man than Marius Mintsingue.

(GLORY hits the portrait, which slides down with a beat, revealing a picture of MINTSINGUE in Oriental drag, smoking from a hooka. She quickly restores the portrait. PIG stage whispers to GLORY.)

PIG. Pssst! The local!

(As ARNGE writes, PIG runs to kitchen, ZARAH from kitchen to boudoir, PIG chases ZARAH into the boudoir, and GLORY runs to the chaise longue, almost leaping over it in an effort to get to ARNGE before he sees what is going on behind him.)

GLORY. Perhaps you'd like to see Marius's scrapbook. I'm sure Pig would be glad to find it for ya.

ARNGE. Yes. That might be very helpful.

GLORY. Pig. *(PIG appears from boudoir.)* Why don't you show this nice gentleman Marius's photos?

PIG. *(Alarmed.)* His photos?!

GLORY. No, I mean his scrapbook.

PIG. Oh. Okay.

GLORY. I can't remember if that old scrapbook is in the laundry room or the garage.

PIG. But it's...oh. Right. We'll look for it everywhere. Let's start with the kitchen.

(ARNGE follows PIG.)

GLORY. And show him around while you're at it.

PIG. *(Glaring murderously at ARNGE.)* Yeah, I'll show him around.

GLORY. Pig. Just show him around.

PIG. Oh. Okay.

GLORY. I'm sure there's a room or two the nice G-Man hasn't seen. *(PIG and ARNGE exit through kitchen. Doorbell persists.)* I'm comin', I'm comin'! Crimeny, you'd think they'd give a gal a second to freshen up between courses. *(GLORY opens door, JOE barges past her.)* Officer Joe. I was just sittin' down for a glass o' tea. Care to join me in the...tea room?

JOE. I'm here on business.

GLORY. Business hours are over, but if you wanna leave your picture and résumé—

JOE. That G-Man been around here? I thought I saw someone come in.

GLORY. Ain't youse two workin' together?

JOE. O' course. I know everything he knows. Only a little later.

GLORY. Well, if he finds anything out, I'll have him get in touch with ya. Now if you'll excuse me...

JOE. Oh, no. This time I'm gonna find out something before he does. Then we'll see who's in charge.

GLORY. Know what you're lookin' for yet?

JOE. Oh, I know. I know, all right. But I ain't tellin *you.*

(JOE looks for clues at lamp.)

GLORY. How about that lamp, huh? It's an original. Only one of its color.

(JOE snoops behind bar.)

JOE. Uh-huh. Who was here when you were allegedly sapped this afternoon?

GLORY. Allege...!? Well, let's see. Allegedly me. But of course I can't prove that.

JOE. Who else?

GLORY. Pig. That's it.

JOE. Uh-huh. Then what's *this*!?

(JOE holds up a copy of Swann in Love, *discovered behind the bar.)*

GLORY. *(Reading.)* "Swann in Love." *(Carefully.)* It's a "book."

(ZARAH enters conspicuously from boudoir in hospital costume. GLORY signals her to leave, and she refuses. JOE suddenly notices screen.)

JOE. Well, who's this here Prowst, anyway? And another thing. What's this thing doing here?

GLORY. What would you like it to do?

JOE. A bed in the living room. That's awful suspicious!

GLORY. You should see where he put the terlet.

(ZARAH clears her throat, gestures to GLORY to introduce her to JOE. GLORY refuses. ZARAH clears her voice more ardently. JOE turns around, sees ZARAH's female side, and is enchanted.)

JOE. Well, excuse me!

ZARAH. Not at all, Officer. Mother, won't you introduce me to your friend?

GLORY. *(Furious.)* Moth...!? *(Simmering.)* Officer Joe, Local Authority--my daughter Mitzi, local color.

(They shake hands. GLORY moves to bar, waiting for the inevitable.)

JOE. Delighted!

ZARAH. Je suis enchantée!

GLORY. *(To ZARAH.)* Hope he doesn't ask for your green card.

JOE. Gee! French! You're not from around here, are ya?

GLORY. *(Aside.)* What a smoothie!

ZARAH. Ah, you *are* a detective!

JOE. Well, not yet.

GLORY. Then I'll save my line about Dragnet.

ZARAH. Why don't we sit down?

(They move to the tête-à-tête, not breaking eye or hand contact.)

GLORY. I hope you two don't mind if I dim the lights.

ZARAH. Pas de deux!

GLORY. Thanks.

(GLORY offhandedly smashes a lamp.)

ZARAH. Mother took great pains to have me educated in France.

GLORY. Wait'll I tell ya about the pains I took to *have* 'er.

JOE. You don't seem like a gal from a show biz family.

ZARAH. Ze theatre is my life. So full of love, romance, passion...

(They are about to kiss, when ZARAH grabs a vase behind JOE and smashes him in the back of the head with it. JOE is unconscious.)

GLORY. *(Panicked.)* Holy Cheese, ya killed the cop. *(Pause.)* First time?

ZARAH. *(Suddenly MALE and murderous.)* Ah, he had it comin' to 'im.

(Knock at door. They react.)

ZARAH. *(FEMALE.)* What'll we do?

(JOE moans.)

GLORY. Quick. Wrap him up. We'll tell him he went into shock. *(Looks at ZARAH.)* ...or panic. *(They roll up JOE in the cover that was draped over the sofa, leaving the book on the sofa. Knock at door. GLORY screams.)* Quick! Get him in the kitchen. *(ZARAH takes JOE'S feet and walks backwards. GLORY takes his head and follows. Just as GLORY is about to disappear into the kitchen, the knock is heard more insistently.)* Just a minute! *(To ZARAH.)* To think I nearly died giving birth to you. *(GLORY drops JOE'S head, which we hear hit the floor with a thud. She runs to answer the door. It is FATHER PAT, very nervous.)* Why, Father, I thought you'd be by about now. We was just sittin' down for some... pigs in a blanket. I'd ask you in, but there ain't enough.

FATHER PAT. *(Pushing his way in.)* I've no time for niceties, Ma'am. Did anyone see me come in?

GLORY. See ya? I'm surprised no one passed you on the porch.

FATHER PAT. The night is filled with evil doers.

GLORY. I bet that's a shock to the both of us. But you like an evening stroll now and then, don't you, Padre?

FATHER PAT. *(Apprehensive.)* What makes you say that, my child?

GLORY. Oh, it's a habit of mine, too. I love to go for a bit of night air...down at the PARK! *(PAT reacts.)* I recognized your voice as soon as you came in, but you didn't recognize mine. Maybe you'll recognize this!

(GLORY bends so that her head is under his chin, and places his hand on her wig.)

FATHER PAT. Mother of Mercy! Pity the poor sinner!

GLORY. Say, don't you guys have a curfew?

FATHER PAT. *(Sniveling.)* I shouldn't be out at night at all. The monsignor would have a hissy fit.

GLORY. Cool your jets, Padre. I'll keep your little secret. I've done it before. Once or twice. Say, how *is* the monsignor these days?

(FATHER PAT takes her hands, throwing a quick look over his shoulder.)

FATHER PAT. May you bask in the glory of the lord for generations to come.

(FATHER PAT kisses GLORY'S hands.)

GLORY. Father, please! I'm a Lut'ran.

(PAT is increasingly amorous.)

FATHER PAT. Irregardless. I know that mourning is a difficult time.

GLORY. If I get to see it.

FATHER PAT. I'm sure your soul aches for support, and friendship.

GLORY. Well, it aches. That's what you're here for, right?

FATHER PAT. Indirectly.

(FATHER PAT fondles GLORY'S behind.)

GLORY. That's pretty roundabout.

FATHER PAT. I know you could use a friend in your corner. Especially if your case comes to trial.

GLORY. *(Pause.)* Yeah, I guess I could, couldn't I? Gee, Father, you're so kind--and *yet* unquestionably masculine. A gal could almost forget you're a man of the cloth.

FATHER PAT. *(Puts his arm around her.)* I forget sometimes myself. Oh, but this is wrong. And poor Mr. Mintsingue not even stiff in the ground yet.

GLORY. Why should the ground change anything? I guess you'll wanna sit down. *(They sit.)* Well, you know, Padre, a gal likes a little stability in her life. A man with authority. A man who looks good in black.

(GLORY moves on FATHER PAT.)

FATHER PAT. *(Coyly.)* Why, Miss Holden. This is most unseemly. What if someone was to walk in?

GLORY. *(A beat. Pulls back.)* You're right, Father. I should be ashamed of myself.

FATHER PAT. I should say so.

GLORY. I don't know what I was thinkin'.

FATHER PAT. And me, a man of the cloth.

GLORY. Someone could've walked right in on us.

FATHER PAT. And how would that look?

(Two beats.)

GLORY. *(Pointing to boudoir.)* Other room's free.

FATHER PAT. After you.

(They lunge for the boudoir. ZARAH peeks out the kitchen door.)

ZARAH. Psst!

GLORY. Oh, Father. I just remembered. I got some wieners to turn over. That collar must be awfully uncomfortable. Why don't you slip into something, you know, tighter.

FATHER PAT. *(Startled, then:)* I'll be waiting for you.

(She pushes him into the boudoir.)

GLORY. Yeah. I'm a-quiver.

(MARTY and EDDIE knock at window. GLORY starts, then lets them in.)

GLORY. I told youse two never to come over here when the heat was on. Hey, you weren't by any chance havin' a friendly game of rockball out by the piazza, were yiz?

MARTY. No. Why?

GLORY. No reason. Whatta yiz want?

MARTY. Nuttin'. We just wanna lookit your "library."

GLORY. What, now? I got all my balls in the air.

EDDIE. Yeah, we know. We figured maybe this was a really *good* time, what with the police around and all.

MARTY. Yeah, we figured with all the heat, you might wanna get rid o' some o' them books, permanentlike.

GLORY. Why, you half-witted milksops! I show you boys the first books you've seen in years, and this is the thanks I get! Now, scram! And never darken my sheets again.

MARTY. I don't wanna sound ungrateful. But you let us look at your books now, or we're gonna tell Officer Joe that you took pictures of *us.*

GLORY. Pictures? *(MARTY and EDDIE nod.)* You know I didn't take any pictures--my hands were full.

EDDIE. Yeah, I didn't hear you talkin' none neither.

(GLORY fumes.)

MARTY. So, you didn't take no pictures, huh?

GLORY. Of course not!

MARTY. How do you like that, huh, Eddie? No pictures.

EDDIE. Geez, Marty. I dunno what to think.

MARTY. Gee, it would take the police an awful lot of snoopin' around to find no pictures, huh, Eddie?

EDDIE. Yeah. Especially if they was lookin' for 'em.

GLORY. I shoulda smelt a rat the first time I seen you guys. I did, but I didn't wanna be rude. G'wan, you know where they are. *(MARTY and EDDIE smile and rush up the stairs.)* And don't stain the Hepplewhites. I just had 'em re-covered!

(JOE bursts past ZARAH into the room, holding ice over his ear, fighting his way to consciousness.)

JOE. I felt a sap hit me hard over the ear, and fell into a well of darkness. "Bite me! Bite me!" she cried. There's nothing like the feel of a woman's teeth against your fist.

ZARAH. Ze Officer has taken a spill.

GLORY. Hey, Captain Encyclopedia! Have a glass of this--you'll feel better. *(From the bookcase full of liquor and unidentified substances, which stands behind the bar, she fills a glass from a bottle clearly labeled "Creme d'Opium," and gives it to him. He downs it, giggles, laughs hysterically, then falls to the floor in a fetal position.)* Mm. Looks "depressed."

(Doorbell rings.)

FATHER PAT. *(Off.)* I'm ready to hear your confession, my pet.

(GLORY and ZARAH struggle to hide JOE.)

GLORY. Oh, Father! I been so sinful. I don't deserve your absolution.

FATHER PAT. *(Off.)* Poppycock, my child. There's no sin so great that penance can't be made... one way or another. Come, and sin no more.

(GLORY and ZARAH stuff a giggling but uncooperative JOE behind the bar.)

GLORY. Just a second. I ain't done yet. *(GLORY slams*

JOE'S head with the Creme d'Opium bottle. Knock at door. ZARAH hides in the kitchen. GLORY answers the door. It's BUDDY.) Ah! An adolescent boy at the door. What could be nicer than that?

BUDDY. Sorry to bother you, Miss Holden. We... uh, I need to ask you some questions.

GLORY. You'll hafta hurry, kid. I'm expecting the Police Boys Choir any minute.

BUDDY. Yeah. Uh, has anything suspicious been going on lately?

(FATHER PAT, delirious, bursts from the boudoir in outrageous leather drag, including but not limited to an enormous black erect phallus.)

FATHER PAT. Take me to heaven, Mother Superior!

(GLORY slams the front door.)

GLORY. *(To FATHER PAT.)* Padre--it's the Bishop!

(FATHER PAT lunges for the boudoir door.)

FATHER PAT. It's stuck.
GLORY. Try that one.

(FATHER PAT opens the closet door.)

FATHER PAT. The closet?
GLORY. Where else? *(FATHER PAT hides. GLORY closes the closet door and opens the front door.)* Sorry to keep you

waiting, kid. Where's your little friend?

BUDDY. Oh, he'll be around. I mean, he couldn't make it. He's not here. What little friend?

GLORY. Some detective.

BUDDY. Gee, thanks! Hey, that's what I came here for.

GLORY. Uh-huh.

BUDDY. I just need some clues! Do you have any?

(JOE can be heard behind the bar.)

GLORY. Clues? Sure, kid. Mr. Mintsingue always kept his clues... *(She looks for available space.)* ...in the chamber. Would you like to see it?

BUDDY. The chamber! Sure!

(GLORY leads the excited boy to the boudoir, and struggles with the door.)

GLORY. You just have to give it a little kick. There you go.

BUDDY. Gee, thanks, Miss Holden! You're the nicest suspect a guy ever met.

GLORY. Think nothing of it, kid. Scream if you need something. *(She slams the door on him. MARTY and EDDIE come down the stairs carrying three large black volumes, and one enormous one.)* What are you doin'? Hey, not that one, you don't know what it cost me. Besides, you can't see it without the glasses, anyway.

(GLORY struggles with them over the book, and PIG leads ARNGE in from the front entrance. MARTY and EDDIE duck in the stairwell.)

PIG. And, uh, this is the sittin' room, but you seen it already.

GLORY. Pig, I'm ashamed of you. Offer the gentleman something to eat. How could you be so *juvenile*?

(GLORY points to ARNGE to signal MARTY and EDDIE.)

MARTY and EDDIE. *(Stage whisper.)* Juvenile?!

(MARTY and EDDIE run upstairs. PIG exits to kitchen.)

PIG. Yeah, I guess I'll, uh, whip up some wieners or somethin'. I dunno.

GLORY. *(Seductive. Gestures to couch.)* Please, won't you...take a load off?

ARNGE. I'm nearly done. I just need to take a quick look at the chamber.

(BUDDY struggles with boudoir door.)

GLORY. The chamber?

ARNGE. Whatever you call it. That room where he kept his props and things. I read about it in a fan magazine.

(BUDDY struggles with door. JOE stirs behind bar.)

GLORY. Well, you can't see it.

ARNGE. I beg your pardon?

GLORY. I mean nobody can. The police locked it up.

ARNGE. Surely I have sufficient reason for seeing it. *(BUDDY knocks on door.)* Is that it? There seems to be someone inside.

GLORY. Those crazy local police! They must've left one behind. *(She moves him to kitchen.)* Why don't we get Pig to help us find the key? Pig! *(PIG enters.)* Pig, why don't you help this lovely man and me find the key to the chamber?

PIG. But it's...

GLORY. And look for it *everywhere!*

PIG. Oh, yeah. The key. Why don't we start wit' the cellar?

GLORY. Better yet, we'll break up into teams. *(She pushes PIG and ARNGE into the kitchen, trying to get them out of the room before JOE surfaces.)* Heck, let's make a game out of it.

(GLORY disappears into the kitchen after PIG and ARNGE. After some struggle, BUDDY forces open the boudoir door, sees that the coast is clear, and opens the window. BOB climbs in, looking pale and shaken. Starts frantically searching the room.)

BUDDY. I don't think she suspected a thing.

BOB. She didn't ask why you were here in the middle of the night?

BUDDY. Nah! I just told her I was looking for clues. Pretty swift, huh?

BOB. *(Preoccupied.)* Yeah. Help me look for something, willya?

BUDDY. Sure! *(Starts searching.)* Hey--why'd we sneak outta here after the gunshots if we were just gonna sneak back in?

BOB. Well, for one thing, we had to change our pants.

BUDDY. I mean besides that! Why didn't we just run and go tell the police what happened?

BOB. I don't think they'd take our word for it.

BUDDY. Well, heck. We didn't do it.

BOB. Yeah, sure, but how do they know that?

BUDDY. Jeepers! Do they know we were here?

BOB. I don't know, I don't know!

BUDDY. Well, how would they know?

BOB. I think I left some... *(Sees book.)* Oh, no! There it is! They've seen it!

BUDDY. Heck. It's just a book. How'll they even know it's yours? *(BOB shows BUDDY the inside cover of the book. BUDDY reads:)* "From the personal library of Master Robert Maurice Anderson. *(Pause.)* If found, please return to 326 Center Lane." *(BOB moans.)* "Levittown." *(BOB hits himself on the head.)* "New York. *(Pause.)* U.S.A." *(BOB breaks down.)* That's a pretty good picture of you, too. Did you draw that?

BOB. I can't believe I did that! Now I'm going to the electric chair.

BUDDY. Gosh!

BOB. My father told me not to read Proust!

BUDDY. Holy Moley! You could just tell them you didn't do it. Maybe your dad'll write a note!

BOB. But I can't go home. I'm a fugitive from the law! They've probably staked out my house by now.

BUDDY. *(Excited.)* Maybe they put out an All-Points Bulletin!

BOB. I'm probably the youngest guy on the ten most wanted list!

BUDDY. Neato! Manhunt!!

BOB. *(Grabs BUDDY.)* Don'tcha understand?!! They're dustin' off the hot seat for me!!!

BUDDY. Don't worry, pal. There's no plausible motive. No grand jury'll indict you without a smoking gun. Habeas corpus says they gotta book ya or release ya. We know your modus operandi--we'll scare up some evidence for your airtight alibi to show you're innocent until proven guilty.

BOB. *(Dumbfounded.)* Oh. Right.

BUDDY. And we can start right here--Miss Holden said all the clues were in the chamber.

BOB. She said that?

(Knock at door.)

BUDDY. We better hurry. C'mon.

(BUDDY and BOB exit to chamber. GLORY enters from kitchen and opens front door. We hear a rush of wind and the spring of an arrow hitting the opposite wall, where an arrow suddenly appears with a note tied to it. GLORY'S jaw drops. ZARAH appears from kitchen.)

GLORY. Indians?

ZARAH. *(Reading.)* "Zis is just a practice shot."

GLORY. Well, as practice shots go, that was good enough for me. He doesn't have to shoot again for my money.

ZARAH. Somesing wicked this way comes!

GLORY. They got Marius. What else do they want? *(GLORY and ZARAH exchange looks. JOE rises, giggling, finds the bottle of opium, and drinks.)* Don't drink that. It's ten dollars an ounce. *(She pulls the bottle from him, spilling some on his uniform.)* Holy cheese! What'll they do if they smell dope on ya?

ZARAH. They'll ask him where he got it.

(GLORY and ZARAH look at each other. Their eyes widen as they realize the significance of this.)

GLORY. Get him out of this.

(They struggle with a giggling, babbling JOE, to remove his uniform.)

JOE. I'm an officer of the law. We know just what we're doing.

GLORY. I'll keep that in mind. Next time they nail me for crimes against nature.

JOE. *(To ZARAH.)* It's a secret. Don't tell your mother.

(In his underwear, he collapses on cot. JOE gags. ZARAH puts her fingers in JOE'S mouth.)

ZARAH. He's choking on his tongue.

GLORY. Hm! Best gag I heard all night.

(ZARAH and GLORY roll him face down.)

ZARAH. He looks so handsome when he sleeps.

GLORY. I promise he'll visit us in Sing-Sing. Get the stain out of these before he comes to.

(ZARAH takes uniform and goes off to kitchen. FATHER PAT bursts from closet, holding his heart and panting.)

FATHER PAT. I can't stay in there any longer. Has the Bishop seen me? *(Sees JOE'S behind and panics.)* The Bishop!

GLORY. Not to worry, Padre. A few tots of sherry and he'll forget everything. Got enough air?

FATHER PAT. *(Panting.)* I think so.

GLORY. Good. Now back in the closet.

FATHER PAT. I can't go back in there! It's rank and oppressive!

GLORY. Yeah. Think about it. *(She stuffs him in and closes the door. GLORY goes to boudoir door, where BUDDY can be heard knocking things over. She goes to open the door. It sticks, so she gives it a hard pull, and it opens, with BOB holding the inside knob, and BUDDY standing in the doorway with armloads of Mintsingue paraphernalia: daggers, bottles of blood, costume pieces, torture devices, et cetera. He may be wearing some: Pince-nez, plumed hat, fake scar, shackles, dagger on belt, and some heavy chains. BOB and GLORY startle each other.)* Artistic! Ya scared me. I didn't even know you was here.

BOB. Actually, nobody's supposed to know I'm here. I'm a fugitive from justice.

GLORY. You are, huh?

BOB. Yes. I'm under suspicion for murder, and I don't even know who. They're probably grilling my dad down at the precinct house right now.

BUDDY. The third degree!!!

GLORY. Suspicion for murder. You must be pretty scared.

BOB. You mean you're not gonna turn me in?

GLORY. *(Almost breaking a smile.)* You just keep diggin' up clues. Me and the police ain't exactly in cahoots. And I don't squeal on my pals.

BUDDY. That makes you an accessory after the fact! Cool!

GLORY. *(Menacing, to BUDDY.)* Kid, don't tell me about accessories.

(BOB looks at GLORY, then at BUDDY. To GLORY:)

BOB. Oh, we were just trying to find...
BUDDY. Clues! Look at 'em!
GLORY. You sure found a lot.
BUDDY. And how! We may have to save some for our next case.
GLORY. *(To BUDDY.)* Say, how'd you like to be a real hero?
BUDDY. A hero? Sure!
GLORY. Have a look at that.

(GLORY gestures toward JOE, who has turned face up.)

BOB. Why it's...
BUDDY. Officer Joe!
GLORY. I'm afraid so.
BUDDY. Is he sick?
GLORY. Sick's a nice word for what he is.

(JOE babbles.)

BOB. He's drunk!
GLORY. Sorry you had to see it, boys. It's a good man's failing. His too.
BUDDY. But he's on duty!
GLORY. *(To BUDDY.)* You wouldn't want him to get caught would you? A nice guy like that. Could be the end of his career!

BUDDY. Heck, no!

GLORY. That's the spirit. Help me get him outta here before the police chief comes down. *(BUDDY grabs one end of the cot. GLORY speaks aside to BOB.)* Willya help me? *(PAUSE. BOB nods. They carry him, stretcher-style on the cot, BUDDY and BOB walking backwards toward the boudoir. JOE'S head is toward them. FATHER PAT runs from the closet into the boudoir, seen only by GLORY.)* Did I say the bedroom? I meant the kitchen. *(They back up toward kitchen. FATHER PAT emerges from boudoir with his priest clothes under his arm, sees boys, lunges for bar, losing clothes.)* Did I say the kitchen? I meant the bedroom.

(They circle around, GLORY leading them toward the boudoir.)

BOB. I think I'm losing him--he's kinda heavy!

GLORY. Yeah, and you got the light end.

(The door is too narrow. They struggle to get through.)

BUDDY. It's too tight.

GLORY. You're just sayin' that. Try again.

(They back up a little, and attack the door again.)

BUDDY. Ooh! I think it needs some grease.

GLORY. Just hold it steady...

BOB. Like that?

GLORY. Yeah. Now slide it in nice and easy... That's it... easy... easy... No, not so fast!!!

(Just as they're almost all the way through, the cot tips and we hear JOE hit the floor. GLORY closes the door. PAT peeks out from the bar, runs from the boudoir, sees the boudoir door opening, lunges back to the closet. GLORY enters from boudoir, closing door. PIG leads ARNGE in from kitchen.)

PIG. *(Shouting to GLORY.)* Gee, I just can't find that key nowhere.

ARNGE. Have *you* found the key?

GLORY. No, I was just tryin' to jimmy it, but *(Shouting to BUDDY and BOB.)* the door just doesn't open, no matter what!

BUDDY. *(Off.)* Oh. Right.

(We hear a crash form the kitchen. PIG runs off to the kitchen.)

ARNGE. Saaay! What happened to that bed?

GLORY. The bed? Oh, we're redecoratin'. We moved the beds out to the terrace for the summertime. We're thinkin' of turning this into the broom closet.

ARNGE. *(Interrupting.)* Perhaps we should call downtown.

GLORY. Oh, you don't wanna do that. Them police a' been stuck in that room half the night. They're probably sleepin' by now.

ARNGE. *(Finding Priest's clothes.)* What's this?

GLORY. Them kids and their crazy costumes. Remind me to have this cleaned.

(Throws suit behind bar. Enter ZARAH from kitchen with JOE'S uniform, leading with male side. She still wears the hospital costume.)

ZARAH. *(MALE.)* It won't come out.

(ZARAH sees ARNGE soon enough to hide her female side, but not soon enough to leave.)

ARNGE. I don't believe we've been introduced.
GLORY. *(Resigned.)* This should be good.

(ZARAH freezes.)

ARNGE. Would you introduce us?
GLORY. Me? Why not. But don't blame me if it doesn't work out. Buck Arnge, Federal Bureau of Investigation allow me to introduce Mr. Mintsingue's... doctor. Doctor...Feygele [pronounced "FAY-guh-luh"]. The world-renowned Dr. Josef Feygele. Doctor Feygele, Agent Arnge.
ARNGE. It's an honor and a privilege.

(ARNGE offers his hand, and ZARAH almost takes it until she realizes that, with her right hand, she'd be showing him her right and female side.)

ZARAH. Ach! Das nicht touchen meine Hants--I'm shterile!
GLORY. *(To ZARAH.)* You ain't sterile, you're just doin' it wrong. *(To ARNGE.)* Dr. Feygele comes to us straight from Vienna, by way of... Denmark.
ARNGE. So, you're Mr. Mintsingue's family doctor?

(GLORY nods yes to ZARAH.)

ZARAH. *(MALE, and inspired.)* Actually, I'm his psycho-analyst.
ARNGE. Psychoanalyst. Really?

GLORY. Yes, Dr. Feygele has the distinction of having studied under Freud and Jung.

ZARAH. *(MALE.)* Well, I...

GLORY. Simultaneously.

ZARAH. *(MALE.)* Yes, you see—

GLORY. On a heart-shaped bed.

ARNGE. What was that?

ZARAH. *(MALE.)* It--it was hard on the head, studying with two such geniuses.

GLORY. Yeah, but when it came to head, you just gave and gave.

ARNGE. That's very admirable. Perhaps you can give us some insight as to what was going through Mr. Mintsingue's mind at the time of his death.

ZARAH. *(MALE.)* A spike! *(GLORY kicks her.)* Ach. Vell, I am very glad you ask me ziss qvestion. Mr. Mintsingue vass inspired, truly a man of genius, but he vass very attached to hiss, how do you say, hiss habits. *(GLORY appears faint.)* Unable to break out of old patterns, he held onto old, unhealthy relationships, the same vay a drowning man grasps an anchor... *(GLORY, behind ARNGE, looks to be dying.)* ... vich to me clearly beshpeaks the pattern of a latent paranoid schizophrenic viss psychotic tendencies. In layman's terms... *(GLORY whimpers.)* ... Mr. Mintsingue vasn't exactly vat you'd call... a normal man.

(ARNGE, triumphant, looks at GLORY.)

GLORY. But then, which of us is? *(Struggle behind boudoir door. All notice.)* Coming, officer. *(To ARNGE.)* Of all the times to remember where I put that key. Why, it's in the laundry room with Marius's diary.

ARNGE. His diary?!

GLORY. Yes, he always hid it in the laundry room. What do you make of that, Doctor?

ZARAH. I am very glad you ask me zis question. Ze almost compulsive attitude toward cleanliness is a distinct sign of...

GLORY. And what a morning this is turning into. Dr. Feygele, you know where the laundry room is. Won't you lead the way?

ZARAH. Zertainly. Follow me.

(ZARAH makes a very big show of going to the kitchen door, and gesturing ARNGE through without letting her female half show. This is so pronounced as to make her walk almost like a hunchback. ARNGE exits.)

GLORY. Aren't you going to ask me to "Walk this way"?

ZARAH. *(FEMALE.)* Did I do somesing wrong?

GLORY. I'm just glad your analysis is paying off. Keep him busy, willya? And show 'im your good side.

(ZARAH exits to kitchen. GLORY opens closet door. FATHER PAT emerges, quaking.)

GLORY. Had enough?

FATHER PAT. You're a vile, corrupt heathen.

GLORY. Yeah, I know. How's that leather fit?

FATHER PAT. *(In an unearthly voice.)* The time will come when the beast shall hate the Whore of Babylon, and make her desolate and naked, and he shall eat her flesh, and burn her with fire.

(FATHER PAT looks down, sees the bobbing phallus, and screams.)

GLORY. Self-discovery. Ain't it grand?

PAT. *(Still staring at phallus.)* Eeeevil! This house is full of eeeevil!!

(He grips the phallus to stop it from bobbing, and scampers back into the closet. GLORY slams the door behind him. PIG enters from kitchen. GLORY sighs. A steady hissing is heard. GLORY and PIG are upstage of sofa.)

GLORY. Pig, you hear somethin'?

PIG. No...

GLORY. Somethin' like water...runnin' water....somethin' like that?

PIG. No, that ain't it. Sounds more like...like somethin' sprung a leak.

(A fuse or magnesium tape burns across the floor, from the entrance toward the sofa.)

GLORY. No, no that's not it. It's more like...like bacon. Sizzlin' in a pan.

PIG. I got it! It sounds like a fuse!

GLORY. A fuse?

PIG. You know, like a fuse for a...

(PIG and GLORY lock eyes.)

PIG and GLORY. A BOMB!

(PIG and GLORY finally see the fuse. PIG follows it to the sofa, pulls a bomb out of the sofa, and throws it out the front door. A prolonged series of explosions, akin to the cascade of garbage from Fibber McGee's closet, is accompanied by flashing lights, smoke, the sound of shattering glass. PIG watches as GLORY, frantic, addresses no one in particular.)

GLORY. Okay, I'm scared now. If you were tryna scare me, I'm scared. Everybody's afraid of you here. We're all really impressed. You don't have to go any further--you're aces with me. I'll vouch for you, pal. You win. YOU CAN GO HOME NOW!!!

(ZARAH and ARNGE enter from kitchen. GLORY remains frenzied through the following exchange.)

GLORY. Oh. Back so soon?
ZARAH. Ze diary vas not to be found.
ARNGE. What was that? It sounded like an explosion.
GLORY. The government says there was no explosion, and that's good enough for me. *(She goes to the bar.)* I was just about to mix up a batch of martinis for breakfast. I don't suppose we could interest you in a few?
ARNGE. Not on duty.
GLORY. Of course not. None of you guys drink on duty. I guess there's gotta be *one* rule.

(A crash from the boudoir.)

BUDDY. *(Off.)* Sorry.
GLORY. I suppose you still want to see the chamber.

ARNGE. You suppose correctly.

GLORY. Now, right?

ARNGE. Yes, now.

GLORY. Well, the only way to do that is... through the window. Why don't we go out around the back way? It's sort of a short cut *(GLORY pushes ZARAH and ARNGE through the kitchen door. GLORY returns almost immediately. Slaps boudoir door.)* Kids! Clear the room. Rear entry!

(GLORY runs to kitchen, followed by PIG.)

(MARTY and EDDIE come down steps with books, wearing 3D glasses. They try to open the window, hear something, and duck upstairs.)

(JOE bursts from the boudoir, pursued by BUDDY and BOB wrapped in clues, and ducks behind the bar. BUDDY and BOB hear something, and run back to boudoir.)

(FATHER PAT runs in from closet, circles quickly looking for clothes, and runs back to closet. A beat. He then runs from closet to window, opens window, climbs out. Window falls, trapping his phallus.)

(Simultaneously, ZARAH peeks in from kitchen, MARTY and EDDIE from steps, JOE from bar, BUDDY and BOB from boudoir. None of them looks in far enough to see or be seen by others. All retreat. A beat.)

(FATHER PAT, after much struggling, breaks free of the phallus, leaving it stuck in the window, and disappears.)

(Simultaneously, ZARAH, MARTY and EDDIE, JOE in underwear and priest's collar, BUDDY and BOB in clues, appear from their respective hiding places. When they reach center, a second before they hit, they look up, see each other, scream, and retreat, as ARNGE appears from the boudoir and GLORY appears from the kitchen.)

ARNGE. Nobody leaves this room!

(ALL freeze. PIG enters from kitchen with plate of wieners, which he holds onto, eventually munching one as he watches the action.)

PIG. I made some wieners, I dunno...
ARNGE. Freeze! *(PIG freezes.)* Who knows what's going on here?

(ALL look to GLORY.)

GLORY. Don't ask me. I just collect the rent. What they do is their own business.
ARNGE. *(To ZARAH.)* Doctor Feygele?
JOE. *(To ZARAH'S other side.)* Mitzi!
GLORY. Where's King Solomon when you need him?

(ZARAH doesn't move or speak.)

ARNGE. Is something wrong?
GLORY. Why do you ask that?
ARNGE. He's not saying anything.
GLORY. That's the Freudian method. I feel better already.

JOE. Baby, say something!

ZARAH. *(Struggling.)* Je suis très, uh, farkakt. Meine shul gibt mir... le mal de mer.

GLORY. These kids today. It's like they have their own language.

JOE. Mitzi, Baby! Don't you recognize me?

ARNGE. *(To GLORY.)* Who's he talking to?

GLORY. Poor Officer Joe.

PIG. He's hopped!

(GLORY elbows Pig in ribs.)

GLORY. Every time he gets drunk, he thinks all Germans are Mitzi Gaynor.

ARNGE. How strange.

GLORY. I'll say. *(To ZARAH.)* What do you make of it, Doc?

(ARNGE notices MARTY and EDDIE.)

ARNGE. Who are you two? *(Opening porn book.)* Ohh! This is the most filthy, disgusting vile... *(Turns more pages.)*... filth... I've ever seen in my...

GLORY. I bet you'll be takin' that home for further inspection.

ARNGE. I'll need to take this home for further inspection. Two juvenile delinquents trafficking in pornography. *(To GLORY.)* In your home. *(Facing BOB.)* And who's this? *(Opens Proust.)* Master Robert Maurice Anderson. The dumbest criminal in the world.

BUDDY. He is not!

(ARNGE regards BUDDY.)

ARNGE. I stand corrected. *(JOE discovers 3D glasses, puts them on. Then discovers biggest book, opens it, jumps back and screams. ARNGE ignores JOE.)* Pig Marrano! Who vied with Marius Mintsingue for the affections of... Zarah Zine! [Pronounced "zeen".]

PIG. No. No, it wasn't like that!

GLORY. Yeah, Don'cha understand community property?

(JOE giggles. All notice. JOE tries to squeeze the 3-D breasts. He looks at others, amazed.)

ARNGE. And Officer Joe. Look at you! Thank God all law enforcement officials aren't vicious reactionary sadists like you.

GLORY. Yeah, imagine if that were true.

PIG. Scary!

ARNGE. With the success of "Crimestopper's Notebook," you would've been next in line for Mintsingue's late-night TV show. If only you could guarantee that he was gone for good!

JOE. Now see here...!

BUDDY. That's the great thing! Everyone had a motive! Even I, a loyal fan, could have been driven so wild by adulation...

BOB. Buddy...

BUDDY. ... that I could've broken in before the show, quietly nailed the escape hatch shut,

BOB. Buddy...

BUDDY. ... crept out, and nobody would've had any reason to suspect...

BOB. Buddy!

(BUDDY stops.)

BUDDY. Oh, Never mind.

(BUDDY sits. Pause.)

ARNGE. Perhaps we should...
BUDDY. It was a good idea, though.

(FATHER PAT re-enters from the front door in his best floor-length dress cassock, wielding an enormous Bible like a weapon.)

FATHER PAT. Eee-vill! This house is full of eee-vil!
GLORY. Now we're really in trouble.
FATHER PAT. The fires of Hell are visited upon the living!
GLORY. Yeah, yeah. Nice dress!
FATHER PAT. Harlots! Painted faces! Desecration!
ARNGE. *(Discovering phallus in window.)* What's this!?

(GLORY, FATHER PAT, and ZARAH speak simultaneously.)

GLORY. Damned if I know!
FATHER PAT. Never seen it before.
ZARAH. We don't have any of those.

PIG. Oh, yeah. That's one o' them...
GLORY. Pig!
ARNGE. It looks like the perpetrator is trying to penetrate our very perimeter. *(Carefully dons surgical gloves, and extracts phallus from window.)* All we have to do is dust this for

prints and... *(FATHER PAT starts.)* Father Pat! I don't even have to take this down to the lab, do I?

(FATHER PAT looks to GLORY helplessly.)

GLORY. Don't ask me. I already gave.

JOE. Those prints don't prove a thing.

ARNGE. They don't need to. I was only bluffing. I'm sure Father Pat has a very good explanation.

GLORY. Well, sure. *(Pause.)* He loves old houses.

BUDDY. Hey! Let's reconstruct the scene of the crime.

GLORY. Why don't we just round up a posse and head 'em off at the pass?

BUDDY. That's a good idea too!

ARNGE. It looks as though each one of you had a perfect motive for committing the murder.

BUDDY. Didj'ever think it might be somebody with no *apparent* motive, someone we don't suspect at all? I mean, our solving the mystery is predicated on the premise that we either know or can know everything, but gosh--epistemologically that's pretty shaky, don'tcha think?

(ALL stare at BUDDY.)

PIG. So how do we find out who did it?

BUDDY. Democratic process--we'll vote!

ARNGE. That won't be necessary. It shouldn't be difficult to see who killed Marius Mintsingue. Mintsingue had turned his back on his family, living a hedonistic life in New York's Greenwich Village, a twisted netherworld of half-men, mannish girls, and hopheads.

GLORY. Gee, I miss the old neighborhood!

ARNGE. On the death of his widowed mother, he returned to the family manor, now a rotting shell of its former grandeur: chipping paint, a crumbling foundation, and the unmistakable chattering of rats like debutantes behind the wainscoting.

GLORY. Debutantes?!

(GLORY shudders audibly.)

ARNGE. But he didn't come back here alone! He brought with him his younger *companion,* a drug-dealing, gin-swilling, smut-trafficking, opportunistic over-the-hill transvestite prostitute, dubiously named... "GLORY HOLDEN"!!

(ALL gasp. GLORY slams bar.)

GLORY. Over-the-hill?

ARNGE. You murdered Marius Mintsingue!

(BUDDY and BOB resolutely shake their heads.)

BOB. Nope, nope.

BUDDY. Couldn't've been Miss Holden.

BOB. That's for sure.

ZARAH. Why not?

BOB. Too obvious.

BUDDY. Yeah, it's never the most suspicious character. That'd be too easy!

GLORY. Thanks, kid. That lets me off. Now if you'd all like to step into the kitchen for some pâté and pretzels...

ARNGE. You forced him into a life of decadence. Trafficking in smut, opiates, and flesh!

GLORY. How do you think we met?

ARNGE. He was going off to make it big in Hollywood, leaving you alone in the suburbs with his furniture, a music box with a dancing sailor in it, and the family manor. You had a fight. You didn't want him to go.

GLORY. *(Through tears.)* Didn't want him to go? I packed his bags!

ARNGE. *(Still pushing.)* Then who was the last person to touch the iron maiden?! *(GLORY glances at ZARAH. ARNGE, surprised, turns to ZARAH.)* Then... then it was *you* who saw Mintsingue last before the show!

ZARAH. *(FEMALE.)* I saw him last before the show, but it wasn't I who killed Marius. It was him!

(ZARAH seems to be looking at PIG, but really at her male half. All look to PIG.)

PIG. *(Mouth full of wieners.)* Me? Baby, how could you say such a thing?

ZARAH. You were jealous. Jealous of me. Jealous of my career.

PIG. You're crazy. I always been very, whaddaya call... supportive of your career.

BUDDY. Okay, *now* how many think Miss Holden did it?

ZARAH. *(FEMALE.)* Admit it! You were jealous of Marius! *(MALE.)* Ha! That's a laugh! Jealous of that old pansy! He wasn't in my league! *(FEMALE.)* It's twue! It's twue! You knew I loved him more than you, so you killed him! *(MALE, frightened, appealing to others.)* The poor girl's gone mad!

Look at her, for the love of God! He didn't want you! Do you know why? He wanted ME! *(ALL gasp. FEMALE, weeping.)* It's not twue! *(MALE.)* Search your soul, you know it's true! *(FEMALE.)* It's not! *(MALE.)* It is! *(FEMALE.)* Bâtard! *(MALE.)* Strumpet! *(LITTLE CHILD.)* Mommy, Daddy, stop fighting. I can't stand it! *(FEMALE.)* Stop whimpering. You sound just like your father! *(Whacks self across head. As LITTLE KID whimpers.)* Daddy! Daddy? *(MALE.)* Mind your tones, you little nancy boy! I'll show you to take after your mother! *(Whacks self on other side of head twice. FEMALE.)* Don't you hit my child! *(MALE.)* You shan't stop me. It's the duty of every parent to thrash his child into seeing reason.

(The two ZARAHS begin to struggle physically, wrestling and hitting each other. PIG hands wieners to BUDDY, who, over the remainder of the scene, eventually eats some, and shares some with MARTY and EDDIE.)

GLORY. *(As if reading.)* Oh! Somebody do something.

PIG. *(Stopping fight.)* Okay, quit it, you two, or I'll hafta separate yiz!

BUDDY. To think, after all this, it was Zarah and Mr. Mintsingue involved in a torrid love triangle. Cool!

ARNGE. I'm afraid you'll have to come with me, Doctor. Time to bid your friends *au revoir.*

(ARNGE puts handcuffs on a non-resistant ZARAH.)

GLORY. Sorry it hadda end this way, kid.

BOB. Excuse me...

PIG. I'll visit ya every day. Well, you know. Give or take.

FATHER PAT. The Lord helps those that repent in their hearts. And you'll have plenty of time to do it.

JOE. I'll wait for you forever, Mitz. I mean, unless you fry.

BOB. Excuse me...

EDDIE. *(To MARTY.)* Do we get to keep the books?

MARTY. *(Stuffing book under his shirt.)* Ixnay on the ooksbay.

(Exiting, ZARAH turns back to room.)

ZARAH. *(FEMALE.)* I love you *(To BOB.)* Especially you, my brave little soldier. I love you all. And I'll never leave you again. *(To ARNGE.)* I'm ready for my close-up now.

BOB. Excuse me. *(Tentatively.)* If Zarah killed Marius, who shot Zarah?

PIG. What?

BOB. *(Authoritatively.)* If Zarah killed Marius, who shot Zarah?

PIG. I was wonderin' about that.

JOE. I was wondering about it too!

GLORY. *(To audience.)* I bet some of *you* folks was wondering about it too.

BOB. *(To ARNGE.)* You acted like you had an airtight case against Glory. But when your case fell apart, you just turned around and accused Zarah.

JOE. Yeah. And how come he knew what was in the music box without looking in?

BUDDY. Yeah, and how come the car pool had to slow down as they turned the corner of Houston and Elm? Anybody could've got a clear shot at him!

(Confused looks at BUDDY.)

BOB. What is it you're really after, Agent Arnge?
GLORY. *(Suavely.)* I think I have a pretty good idea. Hey, Junior--catch!

(GLORY lobs music box over stage, ARNGE instinctively lunges for it, sliding in on his chest, and catches it seconds before it hits the ground. Dream lighting as ARNGE'S eyes meet the portrait's, perhaps electronically.)

ARNGE. Pater? Pa--PAAAAAAAAAAAAAAH!!!

(Lights to normal.)

JOE. This has gone far enough! Who's the detective here anyway?
GLORY. I give up! In the past 48 hours, my husband was killed, *(Points to ZARAH)* two of my best friends almost got her head shot off, I been grilled by 57 varieties of law, a coupla local hustlers are blackmailing me for treasures of Marius' library, some goons are gonna break my legs off and beat me to death with 'em if I don't finish a certain cinema project by tomorrow morning before mass, the local priest has the hots for me, I been sapped, slapped, shot at, bombed, and winged by an arrow. I've had a little too much to drink for someone who hasn't slept in two days, and all's I really wanna do is lie down and shut my brain off. *(To ARNGE.)* BUT I GOT THIS LITTLE MAN INSIDE O' ME, that says there's something funny when the so-called G-MAN says "Au revoir" just like Marius, and knows about a little sailor in a box he never

opened, a box that was the treasured possession of one Algernon Swinburne Mintsingue, Marius Mintsingue's SON!

(GLORY pulls off ARNGE'S fedora, exposing hair unmistakeably like MINTSINGUE'S, which ARNGE grabs and screams. General alarm.)

BOB. So that's why he looked so much like Marius!

GLORY. *(To PIG.)* And you thought they was just savin' room in the program.

ZARAH. *(MALE.)* Marius was married?

GLORY. When he was 30, his parents told him they'd cut off his allowance if he didn't find a wife. He married a debutante from Cleveland. Junior here was born a year later, in time for the divorce.

ARNGE. *(Defensive.)* She divorced him for philandering!

GLORY. *(To PIG.)* "Artistic" philandering.

ARNGE. When Mother died, I hunted my father down. I found out where he lived and how, and I planned a fitting vengeance.

BOB. Wouldn't it've been easier just to... call him up and kind of... talk it over?

BUDDY. Wow!

ARNGE. I knew he could never accept my... way of life.

ZARAH. *(MALE.)* You mean...?

ARNGE. I didn't know there was a name for what I was until I read the Kinsey reports and found out I was a ... a heterosexual.

(General alarm.)

ZARAH. *(FEMALE.)* They lead such tragic lives.

GLORY. He seemed as normal as you or me.

PIG. I knew there was something funny about him.

GLORY. I never met one of 'em that was happy.

BUDDY. Yeah. Imagine having to get blood transfusions every day.

JOE. Let's go, Junior. Time to pay the piper.

PAT. A happy ending after all!

(ARNGE breaks away from JOE, brandishing a revolver. He fires two shots.)

ARNGE. You think you've purged the world of evil? You can't separate murders into random events! Every act of violence is a blow against the oppressive regime of the military-industrial state! Your establishment can't survive, because it's based on the senseless persecution of innocent people, and the wrongful acquisition of beautiful and precious antiquities people of your coarse sensibilities and poor breeding couldn't possible appreciate.

JOE. Whoa-ho! Settle down, Ivan. Nobody's listening to you.

BUDDY. I was. *(ALL stare at him.)* Uh, sorta.

ARNGE. *(Backing to kitchen.)* I'm sorry to end our little party so soon, but I have to be--oof!

(At that moment, FATHER PAT deftly flings the bible at ARNGE'S legs, knocking him to the ground, where JOE quickly handcuffs him. JOE then viciously beats and kicks ARNGE into submission, as MARTY, EDDIE, and BUDDY cheer. They sky begins to lighten.)

MARTY, EDDIE and BUDDY. Yay, Officer Joe!

JOE. Let's go, Junior. Looks like no vengeance for you today!

ARNGE. I would have, though. If it wasn't for you meddling kids.

BUDDY. And don't forget Miss Holden! She helped too!

ARNGE. *(To GLORY.)* You stole from me the father and the furniture I should have had! That music box was mine, and he took it from me!

GLORY. He took it to remember you by.

ARNGE. What?

GLORY. He wanted to come see ya, kid! He talked about it all the time. Your mother wouldn't let him!

ARNGE. Wouldn't let him?

GLORY. She was afraid he'd be a bad influence.

(ARNGE drops his head and thinks.)

ARNGE. Gee. That changes everything.

JOE. There'll be a medal in this for you boys!

BUDDY. Gosh!

PAT. It all goes to show that vengeance is as vengeance does.

GLORY. *(Slow burn.)* Padre, thanks to your moral guidance, this town is what it is today.

ARNGE. *(To GLORY.)* No hard feelings about me killing Dad, and, well, you know, bombing the house, and trying to frame you and everything?

GLORY. Don't sweat it, Slugger. I haven't had hard feelings for years.

JOE. Break it up, break it up. Visiting hours is Wednesdays and Saturdays.

GLORY. I'll knit ya somethin' sharp!
ARNGE. Gee, thanks... "Mom"!

(ARNGE exits, blushing and beaming, ushered out by JOE.)

GLORY. *(Shaking her head.)* Kids.

BUDDY. Wow, Bob--rescued by Father Pat and Officer Joe! Our two heroes!

FATHER PAT. Boys, there's no separation of church and state when it comes to protecting Levittown's model citizens. *(Exits mumbling.)* If only he had used his genius for Good, instead of Evil...

BOB. *(To ZARAH.)* But you said you did it!

GLORY. What?

BOB. You said, "I know what they'll think, and it's twue! It's twue!"

ZARAH. It is twue. They'll think I should have been with him at his last moment. And it's twue! It's twue!

(ZARAH sobs.)

GLORY. Take it easy, kid. It's been a long night.
PIG. Come on, Babe. Let's get some sleep.

(PIG takes ZARAH up the stairs. She stops with a gasp.)

ZARAH. But ze movie! What about ze movie?
PIG. I'll wake you up in time.

(ZARAH looks up at PIG tearily, touches his face.)

ZARAH. Pig?

PIG. Yeah, Doll?

ZARAH. Will I look too washed out if I wear ze blonde wig in ze final scene?

PIG. Ah, you look good in anything.

(PIG and ZARAH exit upstairs.)

GLORY. *(To BOB.)* Kid, maybe I can help you make some sense outta this. There's times in a boy's life when--no. A guy should never think that... Just because a fella...

PIG. *(Off.)* Glory!

GLORY. Oh. Gotta go.

(GLORY exits upstairs. MARTY and EDDIE are climbing out of window. BUDDY is pocketing the remainder of the wieners, and leaving the plate.)

BOB. Hey, Buddy. Wanna come back to my house and have a sleepover?

BUDDY. Gee, Bob, I'd like to, but I sorta promised the guys I'd go to the club with them after the mystery.

BOB. The gu...!?

EDDIE. C'mon, Squirt. We'll learn ya how to fight like a man.

MARTY. Yeah. Coupla lessons from us, ya can beat the shit out of anyone who looks at ya cross-eyed.

(MARTY and EDDIE exit window.)

BUDDY. Cool! *(To BOB.)* Good mystery-solving with ya,

pal. *(Shakes his hand quickly.)* See you in school. *(Goes to window.)* I guess everything worked out all for the best in the end.

(BUDDY sighs, exits window, BOB watching. BOB slowly surveys the wreckage of Mintsingue Manor, and, by extension, his own childhood. He moves to exit front door. GLORY appears at stairs in robe and turban.)

GLORY. Artistic, I wanna thank you for what you done. I'd like to say something wise about everything that's happened here, the meaning of life, how to be a real man, that kind of thing... but I really can't think of nothing. *(Goes to leave. Turns back. Shrugs.)* What *is* a man, anyway?

(BOB looks at GLORY. GLORY exits. FADE TO BLACK.)

END OF PLAY

Cross-Gender Casting of Buddy and Bob,
or
Why the Simon Brothers Use Women

During the writing process and the casting of the original production, we had some thoughts about casting which we'd like to share with you. Now.

We realized that casting real boys as Buddy and Bob would amount to child abuse, considering what they're subjected to in the course of the play. Grown men in those roles would create an air of clownishness, rather than the vulnerability that we wanted. A man and a woman as Buddy and Bob would make their part of the play a heterosexual romance, and we *really* didn't want that. But casting women (preferably smallish women) as Buddy and Bob would highlight their powerlessness in a world where everyone (even other boys) is bigger and more manly than they are.

So we insisted that women be cast as Buddy and Bob (not that anyone argued) and men be cast as everyone else. Casting men as Pig, Marty, Eddie, Joe, Pat, and Arnge underscored their (often misused) male power and authority. We also cast men in the more feminine adult male roles of Marius, Glory, and Zarah, since women playing feminine men would just seem like women.

Actually, we never thought of Glory as feminine, just a resourceful guy in a dress (or harem pants, if you prefer). For some, she so fit the mold of "tough broad" that at least one major New York critic missed the fact that she was a guy. So there's Glory: a hard-nosed dame with a heart of gold. And a dick.

Of course we could have written a play that had some actual female characters in it. Which we're doing. And they'll be played by women. Honest.

M.S. and R.S.
New York, 1996

ACT ONE PROPS

Kitchen Prop Table
Nightstick (SM)
3-D Glasses (2)
Stethoscope
Lone Ranger Mask
Frying Pan
Gong
Small Porn Books (2)   (Marty/Eddie)
Large Porn Book
Ice Bag (Joe's)
Fuse

Prop Table 1
Large Bible
Bomb
Flowers
Book, Swann in Love
Box of clues - teeth, knife, whoopee cushion
Buddy's vest o' clues
Trick noose
Scrap book (Arnge).
Holy WATER
Fake Priest Outfit (On wall)
Powder Puff
Phallus

Back Stage Left
Set rock device
Pat's leather outfit   Hang on hook by door

Back Stage Right

Hospital Screen	Behind stairway door
Buddy Dummy	Behind pip, UR
Strike phone books	
Gun	LOAD GUN!!

Perishables

Fill 2 decanters with water	
Wash ALL Glassware	
Prepare tea/lady finger tray	Kitchen prop table
Fill sugar bowl	
Fill cereal boxes	
Prepare Popcorn	
Prepare Weiners	
Set maiden blood	
Water in opium bottle	

On Chaise

Camera	WIND CAMERA!!!
Trick Dagger	

In TV

Cereal boxes (5)	On velcro
2 bowls w/spoons	Cereal already in bowls
Crazy Straws (2)	
Sugar bowl	
Bag of sugar	
Porno mags (2)	
Severed finger	
Popcorn	
Box of Good & Plenty	

Screen down - Close tubes - Pad & Pencil

Behind Bar
Glasses/Bottles
Swizzle stick
Champagne glasses (2, plastic)   On shelves
Music box on bar (UNLATCH!!)
Ash tray on tête-a-tête table

Under Bar
Bloody glove
Towels, wet (2)/ Crème d'Opium - Preset

ACT TWO PROPS

Behind Bar
Camera (wind!!)   WIND CAMERA!!!!!
Clapboard
Ice bag (blue)
Lubricant / Crème d'Opium
Plate of weiners   Kitchen prop table
Bomb in window seat   in window seat
Load gun   SM table

On Bar
Music box
Book (Swann in Love)
Three glasses
Gin bottle
Cigarettes

On Chaise
Blanket

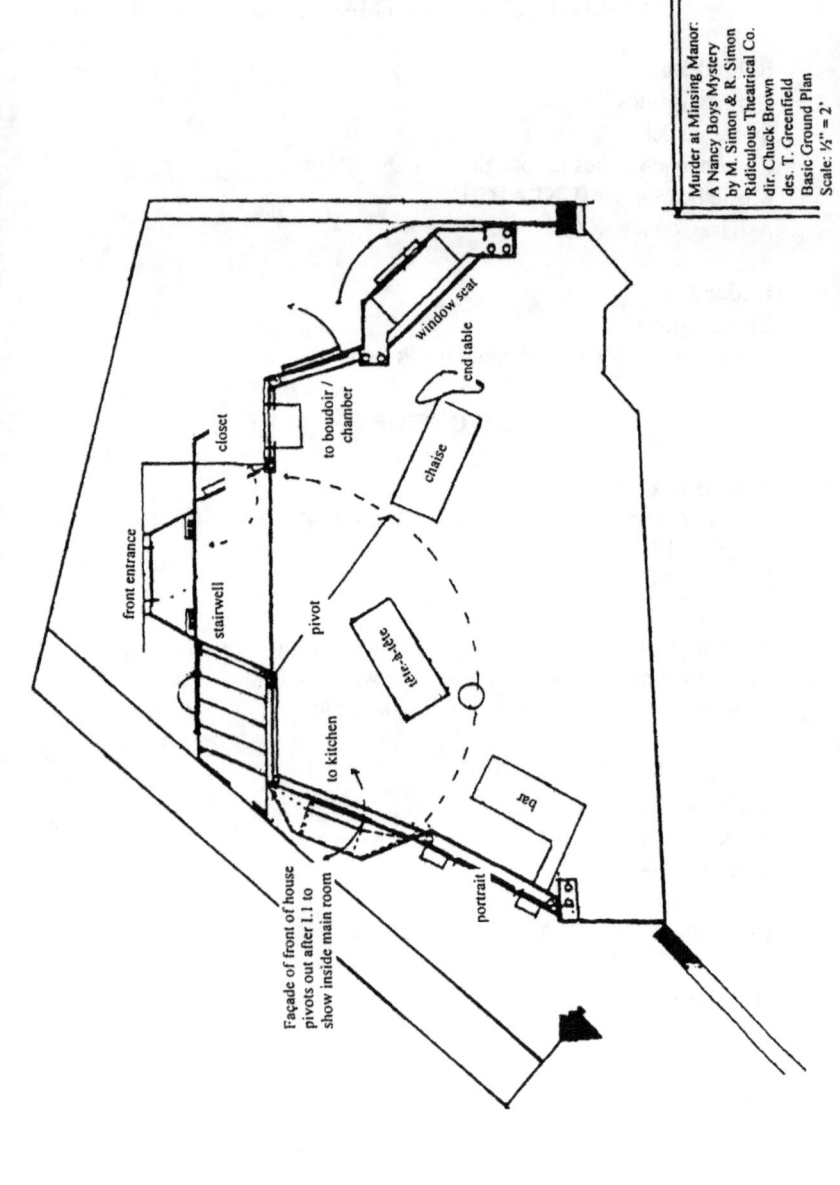

front entrance

closet

stairwell

to boudoir / chamber

pivot

window seat

end table

chaise

tête-à-tête

to kitchen

bar

portrait

Façade of front of house pivots out after I.1 to show inside main room

Murder at Minsing Manor:
A Nancy Boys Mystery
by M. Simon & R. Simon
Ridiculous Theatrical Co.
dir. Chuck Brown
des. T. Greenfield
Basic Ground Plan
Scale: ½" = 2'

OTHER TITLES AVAILABLE FROM SAMUEL FRENCH

...AND THEN THERE WAS NUN

Richard T. Witter and Bruce Gilray

Comedy with Music / 11 characters (m or f)

...And Then There Was Nun is written in the style of a classic 1940's murder mystery; and is a blend of humor and who-dun-it as the actors emulate iconic movie stars of the past.

Take one foreboding mansion on a secluded island, throw in ten whacked-out members of The Holy Order of the Sisters of San Andreas, stir in their unseen and mysterious leader, add an assortment of the sharpest tongues this side of Hollywood and Vine; then infuse with a healthy dose of some of the most famous lines in cinema (slightly warped). Roast well in a preheated treasure trove of movie facts, trivia, legends and gossip for two acts, sit back and savor. *...And Then There Was Nun* is a treat for movie buffs and non-movie buffs alike.

Actors who take on the personas parodied in this play will be creatively challenged to mold their performances with the mannerisms and vocal styles of famous actors of the past, having an amazingly fun experience along the way.

...And Then There Was Nun was the winner of the 1990 "Robby" Award for "Best Comedy Production" and for "Best Actor" – Tif Rice as Sister Katharine.

"...a gas...over the top and as thick as the North Pasture. Needless to add, the audience loved every single second of it."
– *Drama-Logue*

"...the nun's story to end all nun's stories...leagues above most comedies and the laughs come nonstop..."
– *Frontiers*

OTHER TITLES AVAILABLE FROM SAMUEL FRENCH

CAMILLE

Charles Ludlam

Comedy / 7m, 5f, cross-gender casting possible / Multiple Sets

Newly Revised! The landmark Ridiculous Theatre Company production of the classic 19th century melodrama!

Tubercular courtesan Marguerite Gautier abjures her rich lover, Baron De Varville, and sells all her jewels and furnishings to live in the counry with her true love, poor young Armand Duval. Her heart is broken when he agrees to his father's request to abandon him, and returning to her unhealthful life in Paris, she declines rapidly, but is reunited with Armand in a deathbed scene that provokes both laughter and tears.

Originally performed with Charles Ludlam in the title role.

"Oddly touching...one of the most hilarious evenings in New York... worth savoring!"
– *The New York Times*

"Enchanting."
– *Vogue*

"Outrageous."
– *Newhouse Syndicated*

"Very ridiculous, very theatrical, and very funny!"
– *Cue*

OTHER TITLES AVAILABLE FROM SAMUEL FRENCH

DIE MOMMIE DIE!

Charles Busch

Comic melodrama / 3m, 3f / Interior

Newly revised! This comic melodrama evokes the 1960's movie thrillers that featured such aging cinematic icons as Bette Davis, Joan Crawford, Lana Turner and Susan Hayward. Faded pop singer, Angela Andrews, is trapped in a corrosive marriage to film producer, Sol Sussman. In her attempt to find happiness with her younger lover, an out of work TV star, Angela murders her husband with the aid of a poisoned suppository. In a plot that reflects both Greek tragedy as well as Hollywood folklore, Angela's resentful daughter, Edith, convinces Angela's emotionally disturbed son, Lance, to avenge their father's death by killing their mother. Lance, demanding proof of Angela's crime, slips some LSD into her after-dinner coffee, triggering a wild acid trip that exposes all of Angela's dark secrets.

OTHER TITLES AVAILABLE FROM SAMUEL FRENCH

THE SECRETARIES

A Five Lesbian Brothers play written by
Maureen Angelos, Dominique Dibbell, Peg Healey
and Lisa Kron

Comedy-horror / 5f (with doubling)

Something's rotten in Big Bone! Pretty Patty Johnson is thrilled to join the secretarial pool at the Cooney Lumber Mill under the iron-fisted leadership of sultry office manager Susan Curtis. But she soon begins to feel that all is not right—the enforced diet of Slim-Fast shakes, the strange clicking language between the girls, the monthly disappearance of a lumberjack. By the time Patty discovers murder is part of these office killers' skill set, it's too late to turn back! In the guise of satiric exploitation-horror, *The Secretaries* takes an unflinching look at the warping cultural expectations of femininity.

"*The Secretaries* is a sustained, amusing look at the fine line between aggression and assertiveness."
– *The New Yorker*

"The Five Lesbian Brothers render their satirical portraits with a deft but merciless eye."
– *L.A. Times*

"95 minutes of gritty, bawdy, bloody humor pregnant with incisive social commentary."
– *San Francisco Examiner*

"A mordantly cheerful slice of Grand Guignol."
– *New York Times*